BLUSH

Book Two in the Addison-Ross Saga

By KJ Newman

© *Katie Jane Newman 2019*

All rights reserved

ALICE

Time was supposed to be a great healer. That's what pages and pages of google links had said, except there was no link to a website that told you how to mend a heart shattered by your kinky not-an-ex-because - *I don't do relationships, Alice* – former...whatever he was. It was as though there was nothing because that's all the non-relationship had ever been, nothing. Just a blip of madness on the ordinarily dull path of life.

It had been six months since Lucien left the Paris hotel room and there had not been one night where I'd not woken from a dream involving him, crying inconsolably. Time had not healed my pride, nor healed the gaping wound that flapped open in my chest. It really didn't matter how many times I berated myself for wasting emotions on a man who didn't deserve me, the wound didn't close, and the restful sleep didn't come.

Every single day I missed him, and I hated myself for it.

It may have been easier had it been a teenage obsession, but these were not the feelings of an obsessed girl, they were the feelings of a woman who had felt too much, fallen to hard and found herself in too deep. I had become adept at hiding my despair from my friends and I did it so well that they had no idea that Lucien had ever been anything more than my haughty, rude boss. The lies still flowed effortlessly from my tongue and I knew on judgement day I would be heading straight for hell. Knowing my luck, Satan would be wearing Lucien's face.

I hadn't seen Clare and Bonnie from Ross Industries, since I left. I wanted to, they were great people, fun and vibrant, but I couldn't face any talk of Lucien, nor cope with Bonnie's slavish devotion to the very ground he walked on. Every day I thought *today is the day,* the day that I would text and arrange to see them, laugh over cocktails and catch up with the gossip. The masochistic side of me wanted to desperately, but I still felt so bruised and raw that I didn't trust myself. So, I declined their invites and threw myself into my work.

Work was my solace. It had taken over every waking moment since I returned from Paris and I needed it for my survival. I would have sunk if it hadn't been for Xander, the gay love of my life. His belief in me and a hefty loan (Xander was of the opinion it was an investment) from his substantial trust fund provided me with enough capital to start my own business and it kept the roof above our heads. It was small change to him, but his kindness and faith meant so much to me that I gave everything I had to making my business work.

Addison Graphics was slowly becoming a recognised name and even on the dark days, the emails and enquiries made my heart sing. Lucien might haunt the night, but work made my days bright. There was a reason to get up and not dwell on the mess Lucien had left behind. I worked tirelessly and it kept me sane and focused, giving me direction and something finally to be proud of. There was nothing about my dalliance with Lucien that could ever have made me proud.

I barely remember the journey back to London the morning after he walked out. I do remember that the sun was bright and shining down over Paris and that it seemed vicious and cruel to be such a beautiful day when everything had imploded. I don't suppose it had for Lucien, I expected he was wrapped up in the leather-clad arms of Delphine, laughing at 'sweet little Alice'. After all, that's what she called me when she came to visit just a few hours after Lucien had left.

It sickened me that he had turned to her, but it was the swift, metaphorical, kick in the stomach from Delphine, that had sent me plummeting to the depths of despair, lower than I had ever thought was possible. It was because of the soothing tones and the 'Lucien would never be content with just one woman' and the 'better you know now Alice, just how he likes his women,' that I found myself in a peacock feather mask, tied up and naked in a room full of depraved sexual delinquents. I'd like to blame her, but I allowed it to happen. It would have been long forgotten under the fog of the last few months, except I knew Lucien was there that night and the shame was palpable.

He was the last person I'd wanted to see me being led like a lamb to the slaughter, acting on a fantasy I had once told him about. It took one flicker of Delphine's eyes to the balcony above the playroom for me to know that Lucien was there, for me to shout out the safe word and run before she could do whatever she'd planned.

I suppose I should one day thank him. It was grief and anger and the need for revenge that took me to that club, but it was because of him that I didn't surrender my soul. I still shudder to think what I would have done if Delphine hadn't given her plan away, but what ate away at me was knowing exactly why Lucien was there.

Delphine was right. He had certain preferences and it wasn't me.

So, I waited for time to heal me and while the clock ticked, I concentrated on work, building my business slowly, spending as little time away from my desk as I could without disappearing completely into my shell. Life was calm and settled. Xander and I continued to live in my flat, although he spent more and more time with Hugo and less and less with me. His parents admitted they'd known he was gay since puberty, and the change in Xander, for having their acceptance, was a delight. He had finally found his way in life and he deserved to be happy, he was the best person in the world to me although I missed the mess, noise and craziness he brought to my little corner of London. I supposed it wouldn't be long before he left altogether, and I wondered what would hold me together when he did.

I checked my appearance in the hallway mirror as I locked the flat door behind me and trudged down the stairs. It was a bright sunny but cold morning and instead of joining the over-worked, over-stressed throng of yawning commuters on the tube, I opted to walk. I could be late, it was my company although I should have organised myself to be early because it was the day of the office opening.

Addison Graphics was moving out of my pokey kitchen and into an office space in Shoreditch. It sounded a little grander than it was, more of a single-story former church that had been refitted into a hub where self-employed and small business owners could share facilities and cheaper rent. I loved the vibe the moment I walked through the door with the owner to view the available space. It was loud, bright, colourful and filled with people who had so much enthusiasm for their work that it was the right place for me to be. My flat, as much as I loved it, was keeping me away from the world, allowing me to wallow in my prison of misery, and I didn't want to be that version of Alice anymore.

I quickened my step, only stopping briefly to pick up two coffees and pasties. I had recently employed an assistant, Saffron, who was the complete opposite to me with her bright yellow hair, micro minis and tattoos, but the girl had flair and unending ideas with an outrageous sense of humour. I liked her immediately, and it helped that she had a very hot brother who came to pick her up from my flat occasionally. I looked forward to it, even subtly brushing my hair when I heard the roar of his motorbike coming along the road. I hoped he would still pop by now we were moving.

"Morning boss." Saffron called out to me from the steps of the hub.

"Hi Saff." I grinned, handing her one of the coffees and a pastry. "I thought we would dine out on day one!"

"Exciting, isn't it?" She took the coffee and spun the cup, mixing the liquid and foam together. "So much nicer than the flat…" Saffron stopped horrified. "I don't mean that the flat isn't nice, it's just…"

I laughed. "It's ok Saffy, the flat was too small for our impending world domination! This is just the beginning, next stop, the City!"

Saffron giggled and linked her arm in mine as we walked up the stone steps to the double doors. I had to fight to contain the euphoria that was threating to explode out of me, I'd not felt this high since…

Fuck off Lucien.

You will not spoil today.

Saffron pushed the door open of the hub and the sound of people and ringing phones hit us. "Christ alive," she said, "we won't get anything done!"

"Oh ye of little faith!" I laughed. "We will get more done here than we ever did squashed around my kitchen table. You'll see, by the end of the year we'll be millionaires!"

"I hope so!" Saffron said grinning. "I've seen a tattoo…"

"No! No more! You'll end up being the crazy tattoo lady!"

"That's what Zac says, but he's got a massive one on his back, so I don't know what he's going on at me for."

"Does he?" I tried not to let my ears prick up, but I was beginning to find myself waiting for snippets of information about Zac. I knew he was the eldest of her three older brothers, mid-thirties I guessed although I was always careful not to sound like I was too interested in him. Saffron was the baby at twenty-two and she was convinced she was the 'mistake' made when her mother went into a flap about the menopause.

Mistake, or not, Saffron was doted on and theirs was a very tight family unit and over the past month I'd been invited to three family dinners. It was nice. My parents were in Bath and my sister lived in Edinburgh so for us, family gatherings were a logistical nightmare and rarely happened.

"Yeah. It's a nice one too, took months to complete. I don't think he was brave enough for any more, really. He's a bit of a fanny when it comes to that sort of thing. Strange really, given his job."

"Oh?"

"Yeah, he's in the SAS, tough as shit and scarier than you could possibly imagine."

"Military?" That could really make a girl drool. It also made me feel a bit flat. The SAS. It would be another dance with a devil who couldn't commit. I was destined to choose the wrong men.

Fuck it.

We walked through the office to our space. It was an open plan room with desk dividers, high enough to stop distractions but low enough to be involved with the rest of the room. They acted as walls and notice boards, and most of the inhabitants had random arrays of scribbled on paper or pictures of famous people ripped from magazines, tacked on their sides.

We were at the far end, beside the window, with two small desks, a phone and charging sockets. Waiting for us was a large bouquet of flowers and a bottle of prosecco. "Welcome to the Hub, from the Hub," was written on the card. I felt ludicrously happy, I'd made it. Something as simple as office space and an assistant meant I'd made it.

Surely it was now time to move on from Lucien Ross?

LUCIEN

It had been the same dream night after night since I'd left Paris. The accident, the blood, the intense pain in my cheek, the endless, agonised cries. I was being punished again - punished for being a selfish, mindless cunt and punished for what I did to Alice.

I had never lied to her, but when I told her the truth, I kept something back. It was true that I damaged everything I touched, my broken life was enough evidence of that, but Alice had waited to know the reasons why and I could never tell her. It was as though she wanted proof that I was exactly the person I said I was, and I feared seeing the way she looked at me change. She may have tried to mask it, but I would have seen the horror cross her face, and the truth would have eventually cost us.

It tore my soul out when I saw Alice with Delphine. She looked sensational, being led into the playroom, but it was a knife to my stomach to see her there. They were all looking at her gorgeous naked body and I wanted to tear the eyes out of each one of them. Alice must have known I was there because she was out of the club quicker that a bullet from a gun. I wanted to go after her, explain, tell her I understood why she was there, because it was for the same reason as mine – to cover the anguish.

Someone like Alice deserved better than me and I longed to turn back time, to have quashed the pull I'd had to her the day she walked into my office, and just made do with the 'arrangements' I'd had with a handful of willing women. It was easier to have women who knew the rules, who just wanted to play and be played with. I kept myself away from anyone who would fall for me, I wasn't the sort of man anyone could take home to Mum. Isabelle had made sure of that.

Isabelle. I wanted to think of her with emotions other than guilt and regret. She was the one person who would slash me and pour salt into every single wound. I deserved it, I deserved every spiteful word she'd thrown at me. I deserved everything she had done. All of it was my fault.

I wanted to make amends. Fuck, I'd even give her what she had come to London six months ago for, just to make the pain go away, but she'd vanished again. My team went looking, following up leads and we'd even stooped to checking bank accounts but there was nothing. It was as though Isabelle had ceased to exist. I kept the team looking, threw money at them with instructions to do whatever was necessary. There was no way I could move on from the guilt without closure. Isabelle had taken the closure away and the scar on my face was the endless reminder of what had been.

The reminder of why I could never move forward.

I was stuck and I'd taken Alice to hell with me.

I sighed and got out of bed. The apartment was silent, and it was the absence of sound that made me nervous. I'd begun sleeping with music on, just for the company when I woke each morning, but even that had outlived its usefulness.

I missed Alice.

I missed her back chat and warmth and her body, the willing, voluptuous body that was always so open to me. Her face haunted me, the pain I'd caused when I left was all over her soft features and it was the last thing I saw before I went to sleep. The last thing before the demons in my dreams took over. Therapy was probably the answer, but I couldn't face knowing the therapist would likely be as disgusted with me as I was.

I walked through to the kitchen and switched the coffee machine on. I was tired, work was too busy, and I was spending more time in the office than I would have liked. The gym was my solace, but I'd had to get in there early otherwise the girls invaded. It was a boost at first, knowing they thought I looked good, but since Alice, I needed the space and I wasn't getting it. I added a double expresso pod to the machine and waited impatiently for it to complete the cycle. I was relying too much on coffee to get me through the day and whiskey to get me through the night. I was functioning, but barely. I wanted to get the fuck out of my life.

I took my coffee and sat down on the sofa, picking up my tablet to flick through the business pages. It made miserable reading – sterling was low, the threat of recession was very real and the economies around the world were taking a tumble. I knew Ross Industries would be ok, we would ride the storm and if there was no new investment over the next twelve months, we wouldn't fold but the small businesses may not be so lucky.

Then a small article caught my eye. *The HUBbub of London* – I'd deliberately not looked for Alice over the past six months. I knew where she lived and who her friends were so seeing her would have been very easy, but I'd done enough damage and to seek her out would be wrong on every conceivable level. As I read about her new business and the premises where she worked, it suddenly became a pull that was hard to avoid.

I threw the tablet across the room and picked up my phone, selecting a number and pressing 'call' I waited impatiently for the answer.

"Hello?" The woman's voice was breathy and excited.

"Want to play?" I asked.

***

The sexual encounter that morning had left me empty. It was supposed to have released the pent-up feelings I'd had from reading about Alice and her achievements, but instead it left a big lot of nothingness. Rough and emotionless sex had lost its appeal and the sordid fuck in a cheap London hotel had left me with a bitter taste in my mouth. I headed straight to the office gym and worked out until every single muscle burned and my breath was ragged. I wanted to hurt, wanted to feel the pain as my body tried to recover from the pounding I'd given it.

I zoned out, ignoring anyone who came in until the sweat blinded me and I couldn't lift another weight. My PA, Carol, eventually came to find me, cross at having to do so. She was completely immune to me and gave no impression that she thought me anything more than an annoyance.

"Mr Ross." She snapped. "You should have been in the conference room ten minutes ago. Mr Chang has been waiting…"

"If he wants the business, he can wait a little longer." I panted, wiping my face with a towel.

Carol pursed her lips and her eyes vanished into slits. "Really, Mr Ross, it's quite unprofessional…"

"Well, Carol." I said, stretching slowly. "I appreciate you pointing out my flaws however, as I have many, it could take up far too much of your time. Please apologise to Mr Chang and advise him I will be with him in due course. Perhaps you could offer him a coffee…"

"I've already done that."

"Then you have done all that is needed." I chucked the used towel in the wash bin and left the weights room for the shower. It was refreshing to have a female employee who didn't fawn over me and particularly to have a PA that I disliked so much that I wanted to keep.

I showered and took the lift to the conference room. Another meeting, more promises, more stress, more reasons to not sleep, more hours in the office, more time in the gym – except this time I didn't think it would keep the demons away.

Alice was back in my head.

***

Thwack.

The crop whipped through the air and hit the quivering flesh. My playmate gasped, her pleasure ringing in the air, that it was just the permission I needed to bring it down again, over and over until her arse cheek was a mass of red blotches. I felt disgusted. She was dripping pussy juice like a faucet and ordinarily I would have been fucking her until my cock metaphorically came out of her throat, but tonight, I just felt sick.

I chose this life, the emptiness of playtime with a number of willing women, but for some reason this scene tonight had sickened me. It was for the wrong reasons, it wasn't for gratification for her, or for me, it was to forget I'd seen Alice's name in print and to distract myself from turning up on her doorstep.

It made me reprehensible. Angela, whose arse I was whipping, loved it rough, the rougher the better, and she would never notice that I wasn't in the same mindset as her, but I knew what I was doing, and I got lost in my own repulsion. I supposed I should fuck her, she'd been submitting to me for the past couple of hours, it was only fair to finish her off.

Fuck, I wanted a drink. Desperately.

I unzipped my fly and pulled out my cock. It was limp and no amount of frantic rubbing could bring it to life. Instead I used a dildo and let her writhe on it while I tugged at the nipple clamps on her breasts. She came loudly and collapsed onto the bed. I took the clamps from her tits and packed my toys away.

"You didn't cum." She said nervously. "Can I help you with that, Sir?"

"No."

"Oh." She looked at me hesitantly then lowered her eyes. "Have I done something wrong, Sir?"

"No." I swung the holdall onto my shoulder and turned from her. The world I was sinking lower and lower into had become a dark shadow on my life. I was playing the role of a Dom and losing what remained of my soul.

I had to get out and sort my fucking shit before I sank to so far into hell that there could be no return.

I let myself out of the seedy hotel room and hurried down the stairs, not looking back as the chipped door slammed behind me, pausing only to drop my holdall of toys into a skip.

ALICE

"So, I'm having a party." Saffron said putting a steaming mug of coffee down on my desk. It wasn't really a good time to talk, I was struggling with a client who kept changing the brief, and as I'd been putting in sixteen-hour days, I was feeling on the verge of a breakdown.

"Are you?" I muttered, pulling a face as another email popped up. "This bloody client is more trouble that they're worth."

"Chin up, they're paying you by the hour."

"I wish!" I twisted my hair up and shoved a pen through the knot. "What did you say? Party?"

"Yeah! For my birthday. I decided that it's about time I christened my flat and a party would be the most fun way of doing that. What do you think? Can you come?"

"You haven't told me when!"

"Oh! Duh!" Saffron laughed. "A week on Saturday. I hope you can come. Zac will be there…"

"Zac?" I asked, blushing. "And, I need to know this because…?"

"Because you've totally got a crush on him, and I reckon he has a crush on you because he's always on about picking me up. He never does that."

"Oh!" I said trying not to smile. "Really?"

"*'Really?'* Is that all you can say? Really?"

"Ha, yes today it is." I said wearily. "I'm so bloody tired I can't see straight." I downed half the coffee. "What say we leave early and go for cocktails, so you can tell me more about your party."

"That sounds like a plan. Shall I ask Zac to collect me?" Saffron asked cheekily. "He could give you a lift home."

I looked at myself in the laptop screen. "Not today, thanks, Saffron." I took a deep breath in. "I need some air. Can you man the fort for half an hour?"

"Sure thing."

"Thanks."

I pushed the chair backwards and squeezed Saffron's shoulder as I left. I needed to be away from my desk because I couldn't see what I should be focusing on. As with every night, Lucien was my dream the night before and once I'd woken in tears, there was no getting back to sleep. It had been so real. He was there, lying next to me, his arms wrapped around me, so I was cocooned, warm and safe. I should have known it was a dream, it happened often that even in my sleep I knew it wasn't real, but this time the lines of reality and wishful thinking had blurred. I couldn't go back to sleep after that.

I'd done something foolish. It was just before dawn that I found myself standing outside of Lucien's building. It wasn't intentional, I only realised I was there when I came out of my trance. It was as though I'd sleep-walked across London and in the cold light of day, I'd finally woken up. I hailed the first taxi I came across. If the taxi driver had thought me strange for being in an exclusive area of London in my pyjamas, he didn't say anything, perhaps it was the lost look on my face that kept him idling outside of my flat to give me a chance to find my bank card so I could pay him.

I was exhausted.

I thought about Zac as I walked down the steps from the Hub onto the street. I did have a huge crush on him, but I'd hoped for it not to have been noticed. It would confuse my life too much, even though I did harbour rather saucy thoughts about him. In some ways, it made it worse that Saffron wanted to set us up. I wasn't sure if I could ever trust my heart with anyone else. I know Lucien didn't want me, but my heart longed for him and I was still trying to glue the broken pieces back together.

I crossed the road and walked along to the small organic café that I often went to. I needed something green and healthy, the endless cups of coffee and sugary snacks that I had been existing on were not helping my mood or my productivity.

There was a strange feel to the air. The wind was cooler and felt different, as though change was coming. I hoped so, I hoped so much to crawl out of the dark malaise that afflicted me and back out into the light, after all, there was so much good in my life.

The little bell tinkled as I pushed open the door. The girl behind the counter smiled in greeting and I grinned back.

"Hello." She said.

"Hi." I replied, picking up one of the laminated menus on the counter. "I need something green that will boost me to the moon and I'm starving, so the bigger the better!"

She laughed. "There must be something about a cold winter day, a boost is all anyone has come in asking for! Is there anything in particular or shall I surprise you?"

"Surprise me. Ok if I sit in that window seat?"

"Sure thing."

I picked up a couple of weekly London magazines from the rack and took a seat in the window. It was a great spot for people watching and I often got inspiration from seeing the world go by. I loved London with all the sights, smells and noise. It had so much to offer and the wealth of experiences that were available always took me by surprise.

Since Lucien I'd mostly avoided anything that exposed me to the chances of getting drunk and turned down everything I was invited to. It was self-preservation, either I'd end up crying uncontrollably or, worse, I'd end up blabbing the whole sorry saga. Which would have been ok, but Anna, my best friend, had the most successful blog in London and I would end up with a thinly disguised starring role in an article about the broken hearts of London town. A role I definitely didn't want. There was no way I wanted there to be any chance of Lucien finding out that I was still sinking.

I had more pride than that.

I sighed and flicked through one of the magazines. It wasn't the most upbeat of reading, the gloom affecting the financial sector didn't make me want to leap for joy. Owning a small business that relied on other small and medium businesses to give me work, didn't help with the bubbling fear that I would lose everything I had worked so hard to build.

Then I turned the page. Looking up from the magazine in all his smouldering, scarred beauty, was Lucien. It took my breath away. For months I'd been avoiding anything to do with him, never reading the business pages just in case there was even a mention of his name. Scouring the papers for leads was a job I gave initially to Xander, then to Saffron when she came to work for me. I consciously tried to pretend that Lucien had never existed, that our non-relationship had been nothing more than a bad dream that woke me up, like a nightmare did to a child. The more I stared at the photo, the more it wasn't right. His eyes were blank, there was none of the fire that I used to see, his mouth was harder as though he'd forgotten how to smile. It was hard to see the Lucien I still longed for, the man I tried so very hard to forget.

"Shit."

The pain hit me like a thunderbolt, straight to my stomach. *Come on, Alice! Come on.* I closed my eyes against the memories that came flooding back, as though a horror movie was on repeat. The first time, the last time, his last words, his first words – over and over until I had tears running down my face. *Damn you, Lucien, damn you to hell.* I needed to get over him. Now. If one picture could do this to me, what would happen if I ever bumped into him? In a city with eight and a half million people, it was unlikely our paths would ever cross again, but there was no comfort in that. It could happen. What then?

LUCIEN

"Mr Ross, you have an unscheduled visitor in reception." Carol announced over the intercom. I have no idea why she still insisted on calling me Mr Ross, and it was slowly beginning to grate on me. She probably just needed a good fuck to loosen her up, perhaps the smack of a whip on her generous arse would sort her out. I shuddered; I'd sunk lower that I could have possibly imagined to be having those thoughts.

"Who is my unscheduled visitor?"

"A Mr Frank. He says its important."

I felt an icy hand grip my heart. John Frank was my private investigator. I'd hired him ten years ago when Isabelle had first left, and he was now probably the person I trusted the most. I had to trust him, he did lots of delicate jobs for me and he was damn good at what he did. In all instances he always got me the results I wanted but Isabelle was the one case he couldn't crack. She was always one step ahead. Each time he tracked her down, she moved on leaving no trace. It was as though she was a ghost.

She evaded me every single time except for the day she turned up on my doorstep, out of the blue about seven months ago, her arrival and subsequent demands winded me so violently I thought I had taken my last ever breath. I remember the day well, it was imprinted on my mind. It was the day I could have died. The day that Alice had saved my life. I recall very little of my conversation with Isabelle that afternoon, it was as though my broken mind had buried the memories so deep that the words didn't even come back in my dreams. Of course, I know what she had wanted, even with memory loss that particular gem of recollection refused to go. I should have just said 'yes', then this may have been over.

If I'd said yes to her demands, could I have moved on?

Or would I have lost that final bit of hope?

"Show him in please, Carol and cancel all my appointments this afternoon."

"Mr Ross…"

"All of them!" I clipped the intercom off and pushed the chair back. If John Frank had come to my office, he had something for me. He would never waste my time with anything that wasn't concrete. My hands were shaking as I decanted some whiskey into a glass. Even knowing I was heading along a dangerous path with the severity of my alcohol consumption didn't stop me adding a generous couple of fingers.

Sometimes I envied those with a close circle of friends. People to turn to when the going was tough, or I supposed, to celebrate with when the going was great. I wished, so much, that I had someone who could walk this life with me, someone to whom I could explain everything without fear of rejection, and to help with my search.

You had Alice. I took a long drink from the glass, feeling the amber liquid burning my throat. I could never have told Alice any of my shit. I was right when I said that she would never look at me the same if I did. Her bright blue eyes always gave her away, and to see disgust fill them would have given my demons even more power.

I took another large mouthful of whisky, almost throwing it down my throat. I'd let Alice down. I should never, never, have begun anything with her, she was too good for me and the road I took her on was absolutely the wrong one. I broke her, I saw it in her face on that terrible night in Paris and it was the second most loathsome thing I'd ever done.

It's interesting how events can mould a person, from good to bad, kind to unkind, selfless to selfish. I was good once, I laughed, I didn't have the need to beat a woman's arse with a cane… these days everything was now so dark that I couldn't see the light anymore and the blackness was sucking the spirit from me, one sorry day at a time.

"Mr Ross, Mr Frank is here. Would you like coffee?" Carol looked pointedly at the whiskey on my desk. "Or perhaps water?"

Bitch.

"Coffee for Mr Frank please." I replied, giving her a dark look. "And another thing, Carol."

"Yes, Mr Ross."

"I do not pay you to comment, overtly or otherwise, on anything I may, or may not, do is that clear."

"Crystal." I'm pretty sure she called me a bastard under her breath as she left my office to show John in.

"John." I nodded in greeting as the burly investigator walked into my office.

"Lucien." He replied sitting down on the chair in front of the desk.

"My secretary will be bringing coffee."

"I'd rather some of what you're having." John said brusquely. Shit, if he was after whiskey at this time of the day, then things were not great.

I pushed my chair back and crossed over to the dresser where the glasses were, took one and filled it up with whiskey from the decanter alongside.

"Too much?"

John shook his head. "Thanks."

"I assume this isn't a social call?"

"No."

Carol chose that moment to walk in with coffee. Both of us looked up at here with ill-disguised irritation.

"Where would you like this?" She asked looking pointedly at the two glasses of whiskey on the desk.

"Over there will be fine." I waved towards the drinks' unit. She held herself squarely and shot me a look of pure disgust. *Ah, fuck off, you miserable cow.*

"Could you close the door on your way out?" I asked sharply.

Carol didn't reply but the door was closed with more force than I'd expected.

"She's a happy one!" John said with a grin.

"Isn't she just! But as she is a complete turn off, it makes for a lack of distraction, I get a lot more work done."

"You're not going to screw this one then?"

I laughed. "Not this time, but you're welcome to her!"

"She has a face that would freeze ice! No thanks!"

I wrapped my hand around my glass and felt my face pale. "So, the reason you are here is…?"

"I found her."

"Isabelle?"

"Ottie."

"Ottie?" I whispered feeling ice run down my back. "You found Ottie?" My heart thudded so loudly I thought my ears were going to bleed. "Where?" I choked. "Where is she?"

John leaned forward and handed me a piece of paper. On it was an address in France, an address I knew. I was a dumb fuck.

"And Isabelle?" I didn't take my eyes from the address scrawled on the notepaper in John's rounded writing.

"Still looking." I heard him take a drink. "She won't get away this time. We think we know where she is, it's just a question of how we move in."

I wrapped my hand around the piece of paper as hot tears pooled behind my eyes. I was one step closer.

"Thank you." I whispered.

"You alright, man?" John asked gruffly. He didn't comment on the tears that rolled down my cheeks, for which I was grateful. Breaking down in front of anyone wasn't ever part of who I was, but there was no stopping the steady stream.

"Yeah." I wiped my eyes and spun in my chair to look out of the window. "I just wasn't expecting…"

"You lack faith!" John said lightly. "We will find them, Lucien. You have my word."

"I know!"

John knocked back the rest of his whisky and stood up. "I'll be in touch."

I nodded and he left, his footsteps barely making a sound on the carpet. I looked back down at the paper in my hand. France. Why didn't I think…

"Carol." I said pushing the intercom. "Book me the first flight to Nice you can get and find me a hotel."

"You have a very packed diary, Mr Ross."

"It's not important. The flight is."

"Mr Ross…" Carol tapped on her keyboard. "There are a few things that can't be moved."

"Such as." Silently I mouthed expletives down the intercom to her. She'd have to go. I couldn't stand the woman. I'd waited ten years to find Ottie, I wasn't planning on waiting any longer, but as Carol reeled off the list of my commitments, I realised how trapped I was by work.

I was ashamed to feel relieved.

I was too much of a coward to go to Ottie alone.

What did that make me?

I really was a cunt.

ALICE

"You absolutely have to!" Saffron looked affronted as I rejected her suggestion. "I mean, you just have to. I bet if I mentioned it to Xander…"

"Don't!" I said, far louder than I'd wanted to.

"Why not? Because, he'd make you?"

"Yeah!"

"You're such a chicken shit, Alice. You and Zac are made for each other…"

"Saff…"

"Think of all the loaded business owners who would send work your way if they knew about you."

That's what I was worried about. "There are plenty of designers in London to help them!"

"You're being small minded!"

"I am not!" I knew that Saffron meant well, and yes, to be considered for the London City Awards for Outstanding Young Entrepreneur could rocket us to the moon, but I also knew that Lucien was involved in the Awards and no achievement or recognition would be worth that angst. "I know it's an exciting idea, Saff, but we don't have the time for any more work at the moment, I'm working every single hour there is."

"But you could take on another person, or another two people, work less, delegate more. I can see it now!" Saffron announced theatrically. "Don't you want to just see what could happen? I mean, you may not actually get past the application stage, but imagine if you did! How amazing would it be to go to a posh London hotel, all dressed up, and have everyone know who you are. I bet Anna would make you do it!"

"Oh God, don't tell Anna. I'd never hear the end of it." I put my pencil down. "Ok, Saff, I'll think about it."

"Promise?"

"I promise. Now can we please get some work done?"

"I wanted to talk to you about my party. You haven't replied yet."

"I've told you!" I grinned. "Or is it not official if I don't reply on Facebook?"

"Exactly that!" Saffron smiled. Her phone beeped. "Ah, it's Zac, asking what we want for lunch. Shall I tell him you want a sandwich with a side of six-pack."

I blushed and felt the heat across my forehead. Saffron would be the death of my pride, I felt sure. What pride I had left, at least. "Don't worry about me, I'll go out for lunch."

"Zac could take you."

"Saffron!"

"Okay, okay!" She held her hands up in mock surrender. "But I think it's sweet how you both fancy each other and both too shy to do anything about it! I'll get you on the cocktails at my party and you can be brave!"

"You are delusional!" I said, turning my attention to the design I was working on. "Very delusional."

"Look, I know he's my brother but as far as brothers go, he's not hideous to look at and you're all 'dangerous curves'…"

"Dangerous curves?" I said laughing. "Don't you mean chubby?"

"God no! You have the figure that most women would die for. I'd love to have boobs, but sadly I'm stuck with these fried eggs." Saffron stuck her small chest out and looked down glumly. "I mean, there is nothing sexy about me at all. You, on the other hand, are ripe!"

"Ripe?" I snorted with laughter. "Ripe? You've been reading too many cheesy romance books Saffron!"

Saffron grinned. "I love cheese, the gooier the better!" Her phone beeped again. "Too late to run away, Alice. Your knight in shining leather has just pulled up."

Under my breath I said, "oh crap."

I couldn't fix my hair without Saffron catching me, so I just took a deep breath and tried to act cool. Zac had a bag in one hand and his motorbike helmet in the other. He really was very handsome, in a classic kind of way, with a calm manner that radiated from him but while he was gorgeous, he just didn't have the raw sexuality of…

Stop it now, Alice.

"Afternoon!" Zac said grinning. "Hungry?"

Saffron eagerly took the bag from him and he raised his eyebrows at me. I giggled.

"I'm starving!" She said laying out the small food parcels wrapped in parchment. "These are proper old school, where did you get them?"

"From a deli down the road. I hope no one is vegan or special diet or anything…"

"No one being Alice, you mean?" Saffron said opening a sandwich and looking at the filling. "Ooh, ham and coleslaw, my favourite." She took an enormous bite.

"You'll have to excuse my sister. When they gave out manners she was at the back of the queue." Zac smiled at me and his blue eyes seemed to bore into mine. I felt the sudden beating of a pulse that hadn't beaten in six months and I shifted uncomfortably in my seat.

"She doesn't feed me!" Saffron said with a mouthful of sandwich. "Honestly, Zac, it's slavery in here!"

The way Zac was looking at me was making me feel fizzy and hot. His eyes were the brightest blue and the smile that lifted the corner of his full mouth, was really enticing. I had the sudden crazy urge to kiss him.

"I am the worst employer ever." I said, my voice sounding a little higher than usual.

"I bet." Zac said, his grin widening. "Dreadful, I would think."

"The worst." I couldn't take my eyes away. "Would either of you like coffee?" I had to get out of the office before

I stopped breathing altogether. "To go with our vintage lunch?"

"Me please!" Saffron said, ripping a crisp packet open with her teeth. Zac watched her in disgust.

"You are truly vile, Saffron!"

She grinned. "Don't get me started on your vile-ness, brother dearest!"

"Three coffees coming up." I announced standing up.

"I'll walk out with you," Zac said. "I've got to go anyway."

"Did you come all this way just to bring sandwiches?" Saffron asked innocently. "What a caring brother you are!"

"Fuck off, Saffron." Zac said good naturedly.

"I won't be long Saff," I said picking up my coat.

"Be as long as you like!" Saffron replied airily. "I can manage quite well, take the afternoon off if you like!"

"She's as subtle as a ton of bricks." Zac grimaced as we walked through the hub to the front door. "Younger sisters are a complete pain!"

I laughed. "I've got an older sister, she is a pain also."

"Can I buy you a coffee?" Zac asked holding the door open for me.

"Let me buy you one, you bought lunch!" I said, walking through the door waiting for Zac while he closed it behind us. We walked together down the steps and I suddenly had the strangest feeling that I was being watched. I looked all around me, barely breathing as I searched out the familiar black car, but the cars lining the streets were brightly coloured and no one nearby looked like Lucien.

"Are you alright Alice?" Zac asked.

I gave myself a shake and smiled at Zac. "Yes, I'm fine, just seeing things. Work has finally sent me mad." I found myself scanning the street, hoping, and not hoping, that it was Lucien who I was sensing, but there was no reason for him to be anywhere near Shoreditch and I had to stop wishing he would find his way back into my life.

He had made his feelings on that very clear.

LUCIEN

That was the dumbing fucking thing I could have ever done.

I had meant to go to a meeting, instead I ended up in a bar with some sad looking fucks, drinking too much whiskey, trying to shut out the voices in my head. I could hear that horrific afternoon playing over and over in my mind - their screams, my screams - and it slowly began to eat up the remainder of my soul. I should have just gone home, taken a cold shower, sobered up and run my business like the professional I was meant to be.

Instead I went to find Alice.

Dumb fuck.

It was easier that I'd thought to find the Hub. It was a low-level single-story building that may have once been a chapel. A nice place to work, I imagined and with all the people walking in and out, it would have suited Alice and her sociability. I had a such a physical pang for her that it momentarily took my breath away. I wouldn't have gone if I'd not left the skanky bar that I'd found on a shitty backstreet somewhere, pissed. She was walking down the steps with a leather-clad man who was so into her I could almost feel his fucking hard-on from where I was stood.

I wanted her to see me and to rescue me from the drunken pit I was succumbing to, in the way that only Alice could, but she was engrossed in what he was saying to her and apart from one moment that she stopped and looked around, she didn't see me.

She wasn't looking for me anymore.

I wanted to rip his fucking head off. It was primal - an alpha male urge from the Neanderthal that lurked inside every man on the planet. We may have evolved but the cave was still our home deep down and had I had a club, he would have felt it smash down on his skull.

The voice inside whispered that she wasn't mine, I'd let her go, she deserved to be happy and blah, blah, blah but I was too drunk to listen to reason and too sober for it not to rip out my insides.

I should never have gone to Shoreditch, I should never, ever have reopened a wound I'd fought to close. Whatever Alice meant to me should have been left behind in the Paris hotel room and not surfaced right there. I wanted her to be happy, but only happy with me and I'd left her. I'd left her with a look of utter despair on her face. It was a fucked-up mess of my own doing and the consumption of whiskey had only served to make it all so much worse.

I watched as she tentatively linked her arm through his and I felt the green mist of jealousy cloud my eyes and pulse through my veins. It was a feeling I remember from Paris, when she had left the car and gone out with Olivier, to prove a point that worked only too well. It was rage, and ownership, and feral and predatory and completely despicable. I wasn't so much of an arsehole that I couldn't recognise how contemptuous that was. I had no right. No right at all to want to smash him in his chiselled jaw and punch him right in his sparkly eyes.

I knew they were sparkly.

She inspired that in people.

She deserved someone to look at her, like he was looking at her.

She deserved someone better than me.

With my hand gripped tightly around the piece of paper John had given me, I walked into the nearest pub until the voices were silenced.

ALICE

He was so handsome. His eyes twinkled when he spoke, and I found the lightness in his face captivating. Zac was telling me about a secret operation he'd been on and despite the seriousness of the work he had to do, his humorous storytelling had me giggling. I liked him. I liked him a lot. The more we sat talking, the more I wondered if he could be the one to mend my broken heart.

There were no games, no power trips, none of the *you're mine* crap, he appeared genuinely interested in what I had to say, but magnetic pull that I'd felt all the time with Lucien, was missing. I wanted it to be there. I wanted to feel an intense need for Zac, the same need that I had for Lucien and I willed it with my whole being. Zac's face was lovely, perfect even, and in another life, it would be the face I longed to see. He just wasn't Lucien.

It was wrong to compare them, there was nothing about Zac that was remotely like Lucien, he was normal for a start, and nice. Really nice. His eyes were the clearest blue and reminded me of the sky on a bright summer's day. He held my gaze as we spoke and his body language made it very clear how he felt.

He wanted me.

The only question was, did I really want him?

I lost track of time as we sat in the coffee shop, first drinking coffee then moving onto lunch, the sandwiches Zac had brought had been long forgotten. He was so easy to talk to, so comfortable to be with that work paled into a distant memory. It was cathartic to be doing something normal and to be in the company of a man who seemed so uncomplicated. When Zac laughed his whole face lit up and I was attracted to the openness in his manner. He didn't appear to have one trait similar to Lucien so I could forget for just a moment. I wanted to stay in the bubble of normalcy for as long as I could.

I couldn't shake the feeling that Lucien had been in Shoreditch and as much as I was trying to focus on Zac, I found myself surreptitiously looking around just to be sure. I couldn't see him, but it didn't mean I was wrong. I had the feelings before, right back at the beginning of the non-relationship-kinky-sex nightmare that I'd ended up with. And I was always right.

Did I want to be wrong now? The longing for Lucien hadn't faded over time but I had to move on, for my own sanity and because a relationship was still what I craved. It came down to whether my heart would relinquish the grip it had on Lucien and open up for someone else. Could I move on if I was still hoping Lucien would find me?

Zac was talking about Saffron's party when my phone rang shrilly from the depths of my bag.

"Sorry Zac, do you mind?" I asked, retrieving it from the bag. "It's Saffron. Probably wondering where I've been!"

Zac gestured and said, "please do."

"Hi Saffy, all ok?" I asked.

"Alice? There's a lady here. Carol um…" She paused and I heard a voice speak. "Carol Jeffries. She works for…" Saffron paused again and I felt the cold hands of dread pull at my stomach. I didn't need Saffron to tell me, I knew exactly who Carol Jeffries worked for. "…Lucien Ross. Apparently, she says *you'll know*."

"I'll know what?" I asked faintly, closing my eyes. My heart thudded deafeningly in my ears and I wanted the ground to open up and swallow me. Perfect timing, Lucien, perfect sodding timing.

"I've no idea. But, she's here and you need to be here because it's urgent."

"Ok." I whispered through dry lips. "I'm coming." I pushed the call cancel button and looked up at Zac.

"Everything ok?" He asked kindly.

I shook my head slowly. "I don't think it is." I groaned. "My previous boss's PA has turned up and apparently, it's urgent I go back. I've no idea why, or what could possibly be so urgent, perhaps he's lost a password or something ridiculous. I'm sorry Zac, I need to go."

"Just a boss?" Zac asked hesitantly. His face had fallen slightly, and I felt a pang of remorse. Shit, after six months, just as I was beginning to piece everything together, why now?

"A complete pain in the arse." I said with a faux shudder. "Egotistical, spoilt and the sort of boss who expected everyone to ask, 'how high' when he told them to jump." I didn't need the voice in my head to remind me that I jumped the highest of all. Zac seemed appeased by my response, but I couldn't help feeling guilty at the lie. Another lie. Another in the ongoing saga of lies.

I was as despicable as Lucien was.

"I'll walk you back."

"You don't need to." Until I knew how I felt, I didn't want to lead Zac on. He was too nice, too handsome, too kind and too seriously fanciable to be messed around. Plus, it would really put a dampener on mine and Saffron's working relationship if I was careless and I would be up shit creak without a paddle if I lost her.

"Oh, ok." Zac said, looking a little taken aback.

I smiled at him. "Thanks, though, Zac, this has been lovely. I'll see you at Saffy's party?"

"Yes you will. I promised to show my face although, can't promise to show it for long, some of her friends are not my cup of tea at all!"

"Oh hell!" I rolled my eyes. "There speaks the older brother!"

Zac laughed and said, "there's a big difference between the lads of twenty-two that I work with and Saffron's friends! I try to be tolerant!"

"Say no more!" I giggled, "although you would very likely say that about my friends too!"

"Only one way to find out." Zac said, leaning in and giving me a light kiss on the cheek. "See you at the party."

I watched him leave the café and raised my hand to my cheek. There was something there, a slight heat lingered where his lips had been and it ignited a spark of hope, low in my belly, that he could be the one to heal me.

The hope didn't last long.

I arrived back in the office to find Saffron looking flustered and a large, middle aged woman sitting in my chair. She was sipping a glass of water and looking as though there was a bad smell in the air. I swallowed hard and walked into our section.

"Alice!" Saffron leapt up and grabbed my hand, looking relieved. "Carol has been waiting for you."

"Hi." I said, pulling my hand back from Saffron's sweaty grip. "I'm Alice, can I help you?"

"I'm Carol Jeffries, Mr Ross's PA, and I'm very sorry to disturb your lunch however I have a predicament and apparently you could be the only one to sort it out." She bristled somewhat and I supressed a grin.

"I have nothing doing with Mr Ross…"

"I can't say I blame you, Miss Addison, however, he is currently completely inebriated in a bar near here and he refuses to move until you go."

"Why?"

"He's had, and I quote, a shit day and needs you." Carol didn't look like the sort of woman who ever swore. Her hair was too neat, her clothes too pressed and her shoes were far too sensible for her ever to have used expletives. Behind the bristling she looked tired and close to tears.

I almost knew how she felt. Behind my eyes were the memories of the last time Lucien was inebriated, the drunken, broken man rambling his car, followed by the drunken, broken and unconscious man that I found slumped in his shower. I clenched my eyes shut and willed myself to remain calm.

I was far from calm. I could feel the hysteria begin to bubble in my stomach, the gripping fear that something would happen to Lucien and I wouldn't be there when it did. Even though he was out of my life, through his own choice, the very idea of a world without him in it was too much to stand.

"Where is he?" I asked in a dry, flat voice.

Carol said the name of a bar a short walk away and I shrugged on my coat. "You can go back to work if you need to, I can manage Mr Ross." I was cooler and more assertive than I felt. Inside I was crumbling into a heap and wailing to the heavens. I picked up my keys and said to Saffron, "you can go home Saff, I'm going home once I've got Lucien sodding Ross out of the pub. I've had enough of this week, let's take the rest of the week off."

"Really?"

"Yes really! I'll see you on Saturday."

"You are the absolute best." Saffron saved all the documents on her laptop, locked the docking station and was out of the door before I caught my breath.

"Are you sure you don't want me to come too?" Carol asked.

"No, it's fine. He's a pain in the arse but I've dealt with him before, I can do it again."

"Were you and he..." Carol stopped herself. I shook my head.

For the second time that afternoon I told the same lie. "God, no."

Carol smiled and said, "maybe you have the same thoughts as me, then."

"You never know." I muttered, switching off my laptop and pulling down the shutters. I put my laptop into my work bag and tipped the remainder of Carol's water in the pot plant without bothering to ask her if she was finished.

She looked at me strangely then said, "you have a very different attitude towards him than any of the others at the office."

"Is that so?"

"Yes." Carol tilted her head to one side. "It's probably why he asked for you, you didn't fawn over him, maybe."

"Maybe." I walked out with her.

"I have to tell you, Miss Addison, Mr Ross has been using alcohol at lot, he seems to be hiding from something or, I fear, heading down a dark path."

"How bad has it been?"

"Worse than you could imagine. His whole behaviour has been questionable. Too much drinking, spending who knows how much time in the gym, coming in late…it's been building for a while, but this morning he had an unscheduled visitor, a John Frank, I think, and he was completely different afterwards."

"John Frank? I know that name." I wracked my brains for just how I knew it but came up with nothing. "How was Lucien different?"

"He looked like he'd seen a ghost."

LUCIEN

I woke up with a hideous hangover and the taste of stale, cheap whiskey in my mouth. It had taken me a moment to figure out where I was, the last real memory I had was of a rough-looking barmaid pouring me a large whiskey. It must have gone downhill after that.

What was happening to me?

I was always in control, always strong but recently I'd been sliding into a dependency on alcohol and that was a path that would never end well. My father had been a big drinker, and despite being a well-respected banker, he'd ended up dragging us into poverty and I hated what he had done to my mother. I'd promised I would never be that kind of man.

I wasn't. I was worse.

An overpowering feeling of nausea twisted my stomach and I dry-heaved over the edge of my bed. My stomach felt empty and as I pulled myself back into bed, the smell of disinfectant stung my nose. I couldn't have been that drunk if I'd cleared up whatever I'd vomited. I ran my tongue over my teeth. Yes, I'd definitely vomited. Fuck, what a mess I'd become. I was an embarrassment to myself. I shut my eyes tightly and lay back on my pillow.

Not only was I an embarrassment, I was also a piece of shit.

I hadn't always been a piece of shit, but time changes a person and I'd lost sight of who I had been – decent, hardworking, respectful – not now. That Lucien had gone.

I dragged myself up, dressed in clothes I don't remember putting on and stinking of bad booze, from a scramble of mismatched sheets and the blankets from the airing cupboard. I had absolutely no idea why I didn't have a duvet on my bed, and more importantly, no idea how the fuck I'd gotten home. Slowly I walked to the bathroom, but each step was like a pneumatic drill to the brain and I had to lean on the walls for stability. My body shook violently. I had poisoned myself. For all my drunken shenanigans over the years, this was by far the worst one.

I corrected myself as I stood against the wall, forehead to the cool plaster. It was the second worst drunken mess I'd got myself into but this time I didn't have Alice to rescue me from the hell hole, I was completely and painfully alone. My lifestyle choices had left me with no one to call, and the self-loathing ripped through my sweating body. The absence of friends and the agreements with the type of women I'd chosen, had left me with nothing. All I had was the horror that was trapped inside my head. I had acquaintances, plenty of those, and there were plenty of women who wanted more from me, but it was all superficial. I had no one.

You'd had Alice.

I fucked that up, didn't I?

I took several deep breaths and righted myself. The wall had left a cold patch on my forehead that felt strange against the sweaty skin. What a mess.

I stood against the wall scanning my memory for any recollection of getting home, but I found nothing save for one vivid memory. Alice and that leather clad bastard.

I hated him.

Perhaps he is what Alice deserves?

Fuck off.

I took a deep breath, gripped my painful head between my perspiring palms, and took the final steps from my bedroom to the bathroom door. Each tiny movement sent my brain swinging around inside my skull and increased the nausea that I was fighting to keep down. I let out a loud burp and clamped my hand over my mouth for fear of vomiting over the carpet. I slid along the wall and turned the handle of the bathroom door.

It was locked.

The shower was running.

Who the fuck was in my apartment?

ALICE

I hadn't slept a wink. Between Lucien's violent vomiting and the equally violent snoring that I could hear from his bedroom across the hall, I'd given up on any hope of getting sleep and come morning I was feeling unnaturally hot and smelly. Having checked Lucien was still alive, as I'd done every half an hour throughout the long afternoon and even longer night, I stole a quick shower in an attempt to feel human before I ran as far from Lucien's apartment as I could get.

I'd not been able to switch off from the horrible situation he'd dragged me into. I'd actually started to believe that life could become more simple – I was having a nice lunch and a little flirt with Zac, there was laughter and the occasional coquettish tilt of my head, a twirl of my hair through my fingers and then BAM, Lucien blew up in my face and everything went to shit again.

What I should have done was to tell his rather austere PA that I was sorry, but I couldn't help and carried on with my little flirty lunch with Zac. Instead the fear and anxiety from my previous trip to hell with Lucien came back with a force that threatened to obliterate my insides. I tried so hard to keep myself level, to not give anyone a reason to think Lucien was anything other than my egotistical pain-in-the-arse ex-boss when really, I was dying inside, and all the pent-up grief and pain had come back with a vengeance.

Seeing Lucien completely inebriated and babbling with no idea I was there, was almost as hideous as the first part of the dreadful night, seven months earlier, when he had driven drunk to my flat. I was shocked by how gaunt and lost he looked, and him asking for me over and over without ever knowing I was there, twisted my stomach into a panicked knot. His PA bristled and looked disgusted at the state of him which I totally understood. The normally immaculate and controlled Lucien was a bloodshot mess of spilled whiskey and torn shirt buttons. He had chosen the least reputable bar in Shoreditch and while it was a dive, it was also the place he would least likely be found, unless he wanted to be found, of course.

What the fuck had happened this time?

The barmaid, Carol and I managed to manoeuvre Lucien into a private hire, with a huge, burly driver that would help at the other end. It definitely hadn't been part of my plan to go too, but the driver was refusing to take responsibility for Lucien in the state he was in, and Carol looked like she'd rather gouge out her own eyeballs than take Lucien home.

So, it was down to me.

I climbed into the car and looked over at Lucien who was slumped, asleep, against the window. I pulled the door closed and kept my face turned away from him, gazing through a steady stream of silent tears, at the London landscape passing by.

I'd always wondered what would happen if I were to bump into Lucien, would I be cool, blasé, sophisticated, aloof? Able to hold my own, be strong and assertive in the face of his powerful aura? Instead he demanded me, and I went running like a meek little woman only to face a side of Lucien I never wanted to see again.

The worst part was the complete loneliness of that car ride, of having no one to phone for help, and no one to talk to because nobody knew just what Lucien had been to me. My friends were oblivious to me being trapped in some sort of permanent purgatory, paying for my sins, so I couldn't ring up and cry that the love of my life was so drunk that he didn't even know I was sitting beside him.

I stole glances at him. He looked ill. There were deep purple shadows under his eyes, marring the normally tanned skin and I wondered how long it had been since he'd last slept properly. I didn't want to hope that Lucien was suffering like

I still was, I wouldn't have wished that on anyone, but I knew Lucien, he didn't lose control unless something pushed him beyond the limits that he kept a tight hold on. There was a rip that tore through my heart when I considered that it was likely to have been Isabelle that had broken him and that all I was good for was to patch him up for her so she could do it again.

I scrubbed myself in the shower as hard as I could, turning my skin red. The tears came with ease – tiredness and shock sending a steady stream down my cheeks to mingle with the hot water. Walking into Lucien's apartment yesterday afternoon, it was as though nothing had changed, yet everything was so different this time. There were no sordid promises, no whispered instructions, no kinky sex… nothing but the crisp citrusy scent of him. I stayed in the shower until there were no more tears to shed and opened the door, reaching for one of the huge bath sheets in the cupboard.

Wrapping the towel tightly around me, I opened the bathroom door and came face to face with Lucien.

LUCIEN

Alice was standing in the bathroom doorway, wrapped in a towel, looking exhausted. There was no light in her face, none of the sparkle I'd seen during our... whatever it had been. I didn't have the right words to describe what we'd had but it had been more than it should have been and definitely more than I'd been looking for. Alice should never have had to experience the shit I brought to women because she was better than that. I wiped my hand across my sweaty forehead and racked my brain for something to say.

"It's you!" I croaked. Not the most charming way of speaking to someone, especially Alice who had despair all over her face. She'd been crying. The red rims of her blue eyes looked painfully raw and I felt gutted that I'd caused her more hurt. I really was the lowest of the low.

You're an arsehole, Lucien.

"Evidently." She whispered, not looking at me. She shifted from foot to foot and seemed to grip the towel tighter, as a child would with a comfort blanket.

It wasn't the scenario I'd imagined when thinking about bumping into Alice. That was far more X-rated than this painful, awkward experience. From the way Alice was looking it was clear that she'd been involved in my getting home, how else would she have ended up in my apartment? Unless...

Did we...

"Did we?" I asked her, searching my memory for something more than blackness.

"Did we what, Lucien?" She snapped angrily, raising her eyes to mine and glaring at me. "Did we fuck? Is that what you're trying to ask?"

"I...I...I don't know. I don't remember much from yesterday. I don't know what I'm asking."

"I can't say I'm surprised." Alice licked her lips and kept her eyes firmly away from mine.

"Meaning?"

She turned her head to glare at me. "The only thing you fucked yesterday, that I'm aware of, is my day, which was going quite well before I had to deal with you. Of course, what you did before you got so shit faced that you no longer had the power of speech, I don't know. Perhaps Delphine was in town, who knows." Alice shrugged casually. "You likely assumed we fucked because I am in a towel, in your apartment, and I expect you are used to naked women in your home, Lucien…"

"Alice…"

"Just so that you're very clear on why I am here, I got summoned from a lovely lunch, to drag your disgustingly drunken arse home by your PA, who, by the way, was really upset by your behaviour. Not that I'm surprised that she was so mortified, no one deserved to see you covered in whiskey, slobbering all over yourself like some drunken bum. The great Lucien Ross…" Alice shook her head. "And just so you know why I look like this, it's because I had no sleep at all last night."

She laughed bitterly and I recoiled. "Someone somewhere had decided that I'd not paid a big enough price for ever being involved with you and gave me the responsibility for making sure you didn't die. Again. Not my ideal night, I have to say, and if I didn't have to wait for my clothes to finish washing in your machine, because you threw up all over me, I would have been long gone." The washing machine beeped. "Thank fuck." She said, "Now I can get the fuck out of your apartment and as far away from you as possible."

Alice bent down and retrieved some of my sweats from behind the door. "I'm taking these, it's not as though I can get the tube naked…"

"I'll get you a cab."

"I don't want you to get me a cab." She seethed. "I want you to just..." Alice shook her head and I watched as her earrings bounced off her cheeks. "I don't know what the fuck I want, but this wasn't how I imagined my day turning out. Didn't you learn anything from last time? You nearly fucking died, Lucien." Alice held her hand up and continued, "I can't do this. I can't be here. You're toxic. I'm knackered, I've not slept, and I need to go home."

I stood aside so she could leave the confines of the bathroom door and watched as she walked past and into the spare bedroom. I was reeling. There was so much I could say to her, proffer the apologies that were too late, give her all the explanations and the reasons why I was 'toxic' and a cunt and all the despicable things that made me, me. Instead, I stood, leaning against the wall, pinching the bridge of my nose to quell the rising vomit while she banged around in the spare bedroom.

I should have gone to her. I should have told her everything, instead I watched her bang open the door, dressed in my sweats, and storm along the corridor to the lounge. By the time I'd reached the doorway she was stuffing wet clothing into a bag.

"I'm sorry, Alice."

"Save your *'I'm sorry'* for someone who gives a shit, Lucien." She replied sharply. Alice crossed to the coffee table and picked up her bag and phone. Her hand trembled as she reached out for her belongings, and I knew then that she was holding it together as much as I was.

Alice wasn't over me.

So, why didn't I feel glad?

ALICE

I got out of Lucien's apartment and home to the sanctuary of my flat as fast as I possibly could. He had loitered uncomfortably, as though he has something to say but the words didn't come, and I didn't wait any longer than I had to. It was like a bad dream that I was struggling to wake up from, and despite the anger and saturating pain at seeing him again, I didn't take off his sweats when I got home. Instead I curled up on the sofa with a mug of strong tea and the emergency bar of chocolate that I kept for desperate situations and cupped my cheek with the sleeve of Lucien's hoodie.

It smelt of him.

The crisp, citrusy scent that was so intoxicating to me, even many months later. There was a flood of memories that sent tears rolling down my face and caused a pain in my heart so intense I doubled up.

I wanted to be over him so much. I wanted to have moved on to better things, to be cured. Having feelings for Lucien was like an illness that ate away at my insides but there were no doctors to make it all ok. Every time I closed my burning, tired eyes all I could see was him in the bar, sad and desolate, eyes that didn't focus when I said his name. He had no idea I was even there and yet he'd asked for me. Demanded that I be there. I wished I'd said 'no'. I wished I'd never gone to the bar. I wish I'd left scary Carol to figure it out herself.

I leant my head back on the sofa cushion and squeezed my eyes tightly shut. He was still so handsome, still had the face I longed to see every day, still had the lips I was desperate to kiss. Seeing Lucien in a mess again hadn't had the desired effect and cured me, it had made everything so much worse. Zac had been forgotten during those hours at Lucien's, and that morning I felt the bitter taste of guilt in my mouth.

Zac deserved more from me.

I wrapped an arm over my face and inhaled deeply. The scent of Lucien still hit me right in the centre of my body, it was completely breath-taking just how much the craving for him had not faded. It should have been enough to put me off him for life, clearing up endless bouts of vomit and wiping down his sweaty, detoxing body throughout the night, but it had the opposite effect.

The pull to him was unmistakable but I was convinced that he still felt the pull to me. He must have. He called for me once again when his demons tracked him down.

I finished my drink and lay down on the sofa, pulling the hood of the sweatshirt over my head. Curling up in a ball, I drifted into a dreamless, exhausted sleep and when I woke, the sun was beginning to set and my stomach gave an almighty growl.

I hauled myself from the sofa and stiffly walked the short distance to the kitchen. As usual, there was limited pickings, so I made some toast and poured a glass of juice. London was beginning to come alive again, the sounds of the street drifted in the through the open window. It was Friday night and I'd not been out in months, it was about time I re-joined the human race.

***

"Well, I thought you had completely forgotten about us." Bonnie remonstrated as she and Clare joined me in the west end bar. "I mean, we've called and called and you didn't pick up, not once, not even to reply to a text. Do you know how shit that is?"

"I know." I hung my head shamefully. "I know it was deplorable of me and very, very shit and I know I'm a rubbish friend, but I've been so focused on work, this is the first time I've been out since I left Ross Industries."

"The first time? The actual first time? You've not been out in six months?" Clare asked astounded as she shrugged off her jacket. "What the fuck?"

I grinned. "I know! I'm wondering who I am too, but it paid off, work is really busy…"

"Whoopie!" Clare said, picking up a cocktail menu. "That is nowhere near as important as maintaining a social life. You can stay in when you're forty and married with a couple of kids and a cat, your twenties are for being out there, seeing life, kissing frogs… have you even been on a date?"

"Nope."

"I really hope you have a decent vibrator!" She said laughing. "Now, now, now, what to drink, choices, choices!"

"Lucien is being a real shit, you know." Bonnie said, waving at the waitress. "If you thought he was bad when you were there, he's ten million times worse."

"You're over him then?" I asked, willing myself not to read anything into Bonnie's comments. I felt guilty, my afterwork drink suggestion had more to do with Lucien than my friends, which made me more contemptable that I could have thought possible.

"Fuck, no. He is still so divinely smouldering that I literally have drippy pants every time he talks to me. Which isn't very often, he seems to hate everyone. I can't remember the last time we got pastries…"

"I can." Clare said, moving back to allow the waitress to put the cocktails down. "Alice was there. It all stopped after you left, I knew he liked you."

I handed the waitress payment for the drinks and flushed slightly. "I don't think so."

"I do."

"A toast," I said changing the subject quickly. "To living life, being young, drinking too much and kissing frogs!"

"Amen to that!" Bonnie said, chinking her glass against mine. "And to you actually coming out on a Friday night from now on!"

"Sometimes!" I grinned. "I am a grown up these days!"

"Not sometimes," Clare retorted. "Every time."

"So, tell me all the gossip." I said. "Who has been shagging who?"

I sat back and listened as they filled me in on the shenanigans at Ross Industries. My ears pricked up every time there was a snippet of information about Lucien, but the snippets were miniscule. From what I could piece together everyone was scared of Carol, no one knew whether Lucien hated her more or she hated him more and Lucien had become pretty much unbearable.

"Still as hot as fuck, mind you." Clare said, "we all still drool when he bothers to come in. Something is definitely up with him though, he's been an utter shit since you two went off to Paris. I'm not surprised you walked out when you were there, he said to Lana that you lost your temper and told him where to shove his job, that's very impressive."

"Did you see him in his pants?" Bonnie interrupted. "I was literally waiting for you to send a picture and the next I heard, you'd quit and then you vanished. He must have really pissed you off!"

"You've no idea." I grimaced, "life is much simpler now!" It was the truth, until yesterday at least. Now, everything felt complicated and messy. I couldn't get Lucien from my mind and each time the girls mentioned his behaviour the spark of hope ignited a little more.

"I really thought you two…" Clare took a long drink of her cocktail.

"Thought we two what?" I asked nervously.

"You know, were doing 'it'!" Clare grinned. "He was so much nicer when you were there. Now, he's just complete arse, hot obviously, but awful to be in the same room as. He snaps at everyone when he can be bothered to speak and either spends more time in the gym than in his office, or he comes in looking like death. In all seriousness, I think he's ill. Carol said he had a visitor yesterday and the news cannot have been good. He disappeared with no word to anyone, not even Lana, and when Carol came back in, she was really pale and shaky. Something happened."

"It's because he heard I went on a date with Billy the sandwich man, he's broken hearted." Bonnie laughed.

"Billy the sandwich man?" I asked. Regardless of who the visitor was, it would only be Isabelle that could push Lucien over the edge. I hated her.

"Yeah. I bumped into him in a bar, it ended messily. I hide now!"

I laughed. "Nice!"

"Far from!" Bonnie shuddered. "It was so bad I couldn't even pretend it was Lucien."

"Do you really do that?" Clare asked. "Close your eyes and think of him? Christ alive, you're even more pathetic than I'd given you credit for."

It felt nice to back with them, in the middle of the friendly banter that I'd missed during my self-imposed isolation. I'd not realised, until Saffron came to work for me, how lonely I'd been without colleagues. It bothered me more than it should have that Bonnie was still obsessed with Lucien, but as I no longer had anything to hide, the guilt had eased.

"I'd love to know what's going on with him though." Bonnie said.

"Who?" I asked.

"Lucien. I mean, aside from the fact he is the hottest man I've ever seen in my life, Clare is right. He doesn't look well these days."

"Not for a long time." Clare said, looking thoughtful and chewing on her cocktail straw. "Six months ago he was almost fun, he had a laugh with us, bought pastries, and now he's worse than he was before, except he doesn't look as good. I mean, he still looks good compared to most men, but compared to Lucien back then, he's ghostly."

"If I didn't long to jump his bones, I'd be worried about him." Bonnie agreed. "Something has happened. Did you ever get into that secret office cupboard where he stored the head of his ex-wife?"

"No." I admitted. I didn't want to tell her that I'd had the chance one afternoon, just before Paris. She would have a meltdown into her cocktail if she knew I'd been close enough to find out Lucien's secrets. Quite likely it was full of boring accounts and other private business affairs, but perhaps my conscience made an epic mistake that day? Perhaps I should have looked.

Would it have made a difference?

"So, tell us about work?" Clare said, "how's the new venture? Do you want to come back to us?"

I grinned. "Not a chance! Work is busy and stressful, oh my goodness, I've never been so stressed in my life, chasing for business and working every hour possible. I've lost a stone because I'm too busy to eat, perhaps not a bad thing, but seeing my business grow has been a dream come true. Xander helped me set everything up, I couldn't have just stopped being a wage slave if it hadn't been for him, but I'm now in a position that I can start paying him back and I've got an assistant, she's batty but amazing. So, yeah, all good."

"Ah, fabulous!" Clare said. "But, more importantly, what about a man? Any on the horizon?"

I blushed. "I've had a flirt with Saffron's brother, she's my assistant, he's her hot SAS brother, and we had lunch yesterday, but I got called away so…" I shrugged. "I don't know if there is anything to tell, or if there will be. I've not the time for true love at the moment."

"There is always time for rumpy-pumpy though," Bonnie said, "even if it has to be with someone like Billy the sandwich man!"

"If you can't fit him into your life, perhaps he's just not the right man, and all you need from him is a damn good shag!" Clare said thoughtfully. "I imagine a special forces soldier can get in and out without breaking a sweat!"

We all laughed. Bonnie waved at the waitress and ordered more drinks. It was great to be back in the world.

LUCIEN

I couldn't face work, or more specifically Carol, so I stayed on the sofa all day brooding, ignoring the emails and phone calls that I should have really paid attention to. I was taking my eye off the ball so badly that something was eventually going to give - either my health or my business. I was burning the candle at all ends and drinking way too much that everything I'd built would eventually implode. Again. I was mortified and embarrassed that Carol had to come and find me and that, on my insistence, Alice had been dragged into the sorry mess. It was a humiliation of my own making and I had to make amends, somehow.

Carol would be easy. I paid her to put up with me, although her job description didn't include pulling me out of dive bars and I would have to grovel for that one. Alice, on the other hand, deserved so much more than an apology for what I'd done to her. She should never have been caught up in a mix of work and play. She wasn't one of my arrangements, she was too innocent, too kind, too feisty for what we ended up having. I wished I'd kept her at arm's length, ignored my desire for her and not involved either of us in a game that ended up exploding through our lives.

Alice was better than me, better than the lifestyle I'd taken on. Despite her assurances that she enjoyed the kinky sex I'd introduced her to, I knew underneath she needed so much more, and I'd ignored that need to prioritise everything I had wanted.

My hangover brought self-loathing to a whole new level.

I was a selfish cunt.

How the fuck was I going to make amends?

I dragged my tablet across the table, wincing as the plastic backing scraped on the polished top. Switching it on, I typed into the search bar and sent a large guilt-riddled bouquet of flowers to Alice and a much smaller, much less guilt-riddled one to Carol and then lay back on the sofa, switching the TV on.

Automatically the news flicked up. Misery, doom and gloom, talk of recession and the upheaval with the political problems in parliament made woeful viewing, so I switched over to the movie channel and turned on a painfully predicable disaster film that had more than one resemblance to my own life.

My stomach growled and rather than make a meal, I ordered in a takeaway, something I very rarely did. What a mess I'd become, so out of control I didn't recognise myself anymore. It would be easy to phone one of the women I played with, an escape from the self-pity I was finding myself in, but I didn't have the energy to perform, nor the inclination to dominate. I wanted something I'd been burying so deeply under the games, I wanted someone to be with, in every single way a man could be with a woman.

And slowly, the sober voice whispered in my ear, the one I'd been drinking to quieten, *you want that person to be Alice.*

***

"Hi." I said startled, as Alice stood on the top step swaying slightly. "You're the last person I expected to see."

"This is the last place I expected to be." She said slurring slightly, "I had planned to go home, but I got a little drunk. You'd know about that, wouldn't you, Lucien?"

"More than I'd like to admit." I said grimly.

"Well, if I wasn't a little bit drunk, this would be a really bad idea," she said not appearing to have heard me. "I would be at home, safely on my sofa with a pizza, watching a shit film, yet here I am, drunk and on your doorstep, which will be a huge regret tomorrow. I must be mad. I'm going home, forget I came."

"No." I said, reaching for her arm. Alice snatched it away from me as though I'd burnt her.

"Don't touch me, Lucien. You lost that right in Paris."

"I did. I know. What I meant by taking your arm was, come in, have some water, have some food, I've got a takeaway coming and then go home. I can get you a car."

"Why are you being nice to me?"

"After yesterday, I think I owe you."

"Yesterday? You owe me for a whole lot more than yesterday." She snapped, reaching for the doorframe to steady herself. "I've never hated someone as much as I hate you, even Henry was a saint in comparison."

"Why are you here, Alice, if you're this angry and drunk? I feel shit enough, I don't need your vitriol too."

Alice raised her eyes to mine and I saw fear deep within the blue. "Because last time you got that drunk, you nearly died. It's not something that can be easily forgotten, and despite wanting to rip your head off and feed it to pigs, I wanted to make sure you weren't dead." She took a step backwards. "And, now I know you're alive, I can get the fuck out of here, and as far away from you as I can possibly get."

Alice turned from me and began to slowly walk down the stairs. I longed to stop her but the small, unselfish part of me knew it was wrong.

"Lucien?" She asked, turning around.

"Yeah?"

"Next time you get in that state, phone someone else. You lost the right to call me six months ago. Have a nice life." Alice stomped off down the stairs and I stood watching until the front door of the building slammed, rattling the window pain in its centre.

I could smell her perfume in the empty hall. It prickled my nose and with it came a stirring in my groin, the intensity of which I'd not had for months. I wanted her. I wanted her soft body, wrapped around mine. I wanted to feel her skin and taste the essence of her and listen as she made the soft gasps of pleasure. I wanted to make love to her, to feel Alice moving below me, her lips on mine. I wanted her with a feeling that was so powerful my cock stood to attention. It was so hard it was almost painful and I had the desperate urge to run after her, to stop her from leaving. To say sorry and then make love to her or fuck her or spank her - whatever she wanted, I wanted to be the one to give it to her.

Instead, I let her walk out of my life.

It was the right thing to do.

ALICE

Fuck, fuck, fuck, fuck, fuck and double fuck. What had I been thinking? Why did I think it was a good idea to turn up on Lucien's doorstep? Seeing him look so miserable and dejected as he opened the door made me want to launch myself into his arms and not let go. Why did I get drunk, I knew it was a mistake! One or two cocktails would have been plenty, then home with the pizza I'd promised Xander. Instead, argh.

I turned over in bed and swashed my pillow around my head. I shut my eyes tightly but Lucien's face was imprinted on my eyelids and the longing for him intensified. He had looked tired with purple bruises under his eyes, probably from the excesses of the day before, but even so... I wanted him with a need that I could almost taste. It filled me up until all I could feel were tingles across my skin. Would I ever feel this way about anyone else? Could I feel such a desperate physical need for someone who wasn't Lucien?

Were we only supposed to have one big passion? One experience of desire that was so strong that we wondered how we would survive it? Would it be too dangerous for our souls if we were to have it for too long? Passion died, right? That's what the books said – find someone you can be friends with, someone to grow old with, someone with whom sex and the intensity of physical feelings was only part of what made you and them a whole being.

Surely there could be no happy ending with someone who make your brain fizz?

There was a knock at the door, and I waited for Xander to open it. When the knock came again, I realised Xander must have either left early or not come back from wherever he went yesterday. I dragged my dishevelled self from the warmth of my bed and without bothering to check my appearance in the mirror, I crossed my flat and opened the door.

The delivery man was hidden by the enormous bouquet of flowers he was holding. I knew immediately who they were from and churlishly I wanted to tell the man to take them back. It was only because the blooms were so large and he'd clearly struggled up the stairs with them, that I stood aside for him to stagger in. By anyone's standards it was a ridiculous bouquet for an apology and if Lucien thought I'd be impressed by a display of wealth such as those exotic flowers, then he had no idea of who I really was.

The delivery man set the flowers down on the floor, with difficulty and looked red faced and sweaty as he came from behind them.

"Thank you." I said.

He merely grunted at me and walked out of my flat. I sat down on the sofa and looked at the flowers. I didn't have enough vases, enough room or enough table space for the number of stems in the bouquet. I took the card from the envelope *I'm so sorry, I'm so sorry for everything. Lx* and clutched it to my chest. *Sorry* wasn't what I wanted but what I wanted, I would never have.

I reached for my phone and began typing a text, before having second thoughts and throwing it onto the sofa where I left it for the day.

***

"You came and you look fabulous!" Saffron said, swinging the door open and enveloping me in an inebriated hug. "Zac's here, says he's not staying long, my friends are arseholes apparently, I think he's waiting to see you. I see love on the horizon!"

"Saffron!" I said, brandishing two bottles of prosecco. "Shush up, will you!"

"Don't be embarrassed, I'd love you for a sister in law, you're the coolest. Thanks for the bottles, you can put them in the kitchen if you like, it's become the bar! Come and meet everyone, unless you are really only here to see Zac, in which case he's in the lounge looking mean and moody."

Saffron slammed the door and dragged me by the arm into the throng of people. "Everyone!" She yelled, "this is Alice, my boss, she's fabulous, look after her and don't tell her the shameful things you know about me, I love my job."

I waved embarrassedly at everyone and stole my way through the sea of people to the kitchen where I found a clean glass and popped the cork on one of the prosecco bottles.

"Five minutes, Alice. Just stay for five minutes." I said to myself as I was jostled around the small kitchen. Saffron's flat, as lovely as it was, made my flat seem palatial and there were too many people there for comfort. The air was hot and sweaty and everywhere I turned, I bumped into someone.

"Not your idea of fun either?" The soft voice of Zac said into my ear.

I smiled tightly. "I'm a little too hungover for this many people." I admitted. "I accidentally met some former colleagues last night and they coerced me into having too many cocktails. I'm feeling it today!"

Zac leaned in to me to let someone squeeze past. "How long do you think you can stand?"

"About five more minutes." Someone pushed past me and I banged my hip on the table. "Ouch! Perhaps one more minute! I've not been out for six months, this is one step too far into a social life for me!"

Zac grinned. "I know the feeling. Fancy getting a drink somewhere a little roomier?"

"You're on!"

Saffron pushed her way towards us and said, "do you both have a drink?"

I gestured with my glass. "Yes, Saff, we're fine here."

"Ah," she said, squeezing both our arms, "you two would make a fine couple."

"For fuck's sake, Saff." Zac muttered.

"What?" She asked innocently, "you both like each other, go for it." Saffron took the open bottle from the table and drank from it. "Have fun, mingle, whatever…" and with the bottle firmly in her grip, she disappeared towards the small lounge.

Zac and I avoided looking at each other.

"Well that was embarrassing." He said finally. "Sorry about my sister."

I put my glass down on the table. "She's just hyper, this party has been a big deal to her, I think a boy may be involved! She's been speaking about someone a lot, Tyler I think." I got bumped again. "Sorry Zac, I can't cope with this, I've been too out of the social scene for too long, I'm going to go."

"Do you fancy a drink?"

I wanted to say no. I wanted to go home and deal with the rainforest in my lounge and brood over Lucien and his drunken antics. Instead I said, "Yes, that would be great."

Zac pushed his way towards the door and I followed, bumping into Saffron's friends as I jostled my way past them. As soon as we were outside the flat, I relaxed and felt the cool evening air brush over my sweaty skin.

"Oh, that feels better already." I said, tipping my head up and closing my eyes. "I think I've inhaled more than enough sweat for one evening!"

"Yeah, not my idea of a good time, I only went because…" Zac stopped himself and took my arm to cross the road.

"Because?"

"I wanted to see you." He said simply.

"Oh." I whispered, looking down at the road. It would be so simple to fall for Zac, someone handsome and kind with a hot, heroic job. I wanted to. Right there and then in the middle of a busy street in London, I wanted to fall head over heels for him. I could feel the muscles in his biceps digging into my arm as he guided me across the road. There was something between us, but I wasn't sure it was enough to banish Lucien from my thoughts. He'd been in my mind all day, exactly where I didn't want him to be. I had hoped he would have given me some form of explanation for his behaviour, but I was drunk and he said nothing and now he was in my head and it was driving me insane.

Zac stopped to look at me. "Not the response I was hoping for!" He said with a light smile. It didn't reach his eyes and I felt terrible.

"Sorry, I've been in self-imposed social isolation for some time and I've forgotten how to interact." I said to him. "It's been all work and no play that I'm now painfully awkward and a bit rubbish really!"

"That's ok." He said, not looking as though it was ok.

"Can we try that again?" I asked, linking arms with his and walking away from the crossing. It felt strange, slightly unnatural and forced but I kept a smile on my face despite the longing for Lucien intensifying. It all felt exactly right with Lucien, I didn't have to force anything or pretend, apart from hiding my feelings from him, of course. I wanted to really like Zac and I hated that my feelings for Lucien could ruin whatever could be between Zac and me.

Zac gestured towards a bar. "Shall we try there? It doesn't look too hot and sweaty and I don't know about you, but I could murder a cold pint."

"Looks good to me." He held the door open for me and I walked into the cool, air-conditioned bar.

LUCIEN

I watched Alice walk into the bar with the same man she was with the other day. She looked uncertain, nervous almost, as though she didn't really want to be with him. She linked arms with him, and he smiled down at her, and the Neanderthal within me wanted to run across the road and smash his face in.

It wasn't me. I had never been someone with aggressive thoughts – yes, I was assertive and forceful in business and dominant in the bedroom, but violence was never apart of who I was.

Until now. Now, I didn't know who the fuck I was.

The urge to go drinking swept over me like a wave. I tightened my grip on the address John had given me, that I took everywhere with me in my pocket. It was a talisman I held onto and for the millionth time I wondered how I was going to find the courage to go to Ottie. Just thinking about her made me want to crumple into a heap. I had failed everyone I'd ever cared about, and unless John came up with the goods, there was no way of ever apologising for the mistakes of the past.

I owed so much.

I stood outside the bar and looked in at Alice. She wasn't sure about him, there was so much that gave her away, or perhaps I just knew her too well. I saw the signs, she couldn't keep eye contact, she looked around her, she fiddled with her wine glass – it didn't need a psychologist to see that she wasn't as comfortable as perhaps she wanted to be. His body language was too easy to read, and I clenched my fists tightly until my knuckles turned white. He wanted her. He wanted her so badly that he was blinded to her almost indifference but for the first time in my life, I believed I was going to lose, and I would do anything I could for that not to happen.

I sat in a coffee shop across the road from the bar and nursed a bitter, lukewarm coffee. It did nothing to help my mind switch off, but I refused to go down the alcohol route again, this time I had to keep absolute control. There was no more handing it over to the voices in my head, I had to begin to repair the damage I'd caused. One day John would find Isabelle and I could resolve all that, but until then, I had to make amends with Alice.

I was utterly convinced that the only person in the world who could save me from the demons in my head, was her. My feelings for Alice had surfaced and the longer I watched her in the bar, the surer I was that I could win her back.

I would not lose her to another man, but I had to tell her that I made a mistake and that I was sorrier that she would ever know. I had to tell her properly, not with a mountain of flowers or anything similarly pathetic that I could hide behind. No, this time, to make Alice believe I was telling her the truth, it had to be from the heart.

And that was the most frightening part of all.

ALICE

Zac was so hot. Smoking hot. The more we talked the more I liked him but the more I felt something wasn't quite right. He made me laugh, he was delicious to look at and a few times I caught myself wondering what he'd be like in bed. For all his muscles and badass job and the saving-the-world stuff he'd told me very little about, I couldn't help but think he would be nice. Not explosive or dominant or creative, just nice. Perhaps I needed nice, perhaps I needed someone who didn't want to play games, or leave in the middle of the night, or fuck big breasted sluts with a coke problem, perhaps nice was where I should be headed.

It's just nice seemed a little dull.

I wanted fireworks and passion and the desperate need to be part of something magical. I needed sparks and the insane can't-live-without-them connection that took one's breath away. I should not have gone to Lucien's yesterday, I should have left well alone. I couldn't dance with the Devil again because I wouldn't survive another *non-relationship*, I needed to be the centre of someone's world and the way Zac was looking at me, I could be just that.

Which made me a complete bitch.

Would second best ever be enough?

I wasn't a bad person, I deserved to be happy and Zac was sweet and sexy and just the sort of person who would make me happy. I adored his family, they liked me, it could be a perfect match.

He placed his hand over mine and moved closer to speak to me. I held my breath, waiting for a spark to ignite, waiting for a bolt straight to the centre of me. I smiled at him and something flickered, it was only there for a moment, but a moment was all that I needed. I leant in, kissed Zac and waited for the boom.

LUCIEN

She kissed him.
She.
Kissed.
Him.

There was anguish and rage and a green mist that blinded me. There was a voice telling me it was my fault, that it was always my fault, that I fucked everything, and I deserved this.

I chucked ten pounds down onto the table and left the café, my one intent was to beat his brains in until I hailed a cab and gave the address of a hotel I knew only too well. Sending a message on my phone, I sat back in the seat and watched London pass by. I diverted the cab to my street and left it idling on the road until I collected my remaining toys.

The only way to avoid slipping into a bottle of whiskey was to fuck and fuck hard.

Angela was already at the hotel, meekly kneeling naked on the floor of the room. It was a seedy hotel but they asked no questions and were always happy to take a wedge of cash in exchange for no registration form. I closed the door of the room and dropped my bag on the floor.

"The safe word is Green." I barked. "You will do what I say and if you don't, you will be punished. Do you understand?"

"Yes Sir."

"And the safe word?"

"Green Sir."

I shut my eyes to the voice telling me to go to Alice and instead I went to the small shower room and freshened myself up. I hadn't planned to return to these sexual games, I'd wanted to step away from it all and because of that, I had thrown many of my toys away. Seeing Alice kissing that bastard had made me see red and I needed a controlled way to release that rage.

I finished my wash and went back into the bedroom. Angela had her eyes gazing down and her chest raised for me.

"Turn over, raise your arse." I said sharply. Angela did as I asked. Her pussy was swollen, ready and open for me. I looked at the bag of toys and back to her, knowing she wanted my crop on her flesh. It made me feel sick.

I couldn't do it. I was there for all the wrong reasons and it was unfair on both of us. Angela needed more than I could give her, she needed a Dom who would respect the rules and there was a doubt in me that I wouldn't stop if things went too far.

More than that, she wasn't Alice.

Fuck.

"I'm sorry, Angela." I said, picking up the bag. "I can't do this. Go home."

"Sir?"

"You'll need to find someone else to play with."

"Sir?" She asked sitting up, her lower lip quivering, "are you displeased with me"?

"Not you, me. This is about me." I cupped her cheek with my hand. "This scene, these games, this type of sex is no longer what I need. I thought it was what I wanted when I came here, but I can't do it anymore. I'm sorry." I handed her some notes from my wallet. "Get a cab home. I'm sorry."

Angela wrapped her hand around the notes and a lone tear rolled down her cheek. "Did I do something?"

I knelt down before her. "You are a great play-mate but I've changed. I don't want this lifestyle anymore, there is too much at stake for me to do this any longer. You will find another Dom to play with, and he will deserve your submission. I never wanted to be a Dom, it was a reaction to something that happened a long time ago. This isn't me. I don't want this, and you deserve someone who can focus on you and your needs, not someone like me who wants somebody else and uses you to forget."

I gently kissed her cheek and left the room, binning the final bag of toys in the skip at the back of the hotel. I was free of that burden, so what now?

ALICE

Zac was clearly waiting for an invitation to come home with me, as he loitered at the underground gate. I'd had enough wine that the words would have slipped off my tongue easily, but something held me back. The kiss, while nice, had not lit me up with sunbeams and to take him home would have confused things. I needed to think and leading Zac on before I was ready to make a decision, wouldn't make me the person I wanted to be.

"I had a great evening, thank you." I said, retrieving my oyster card from the bottom of my bag.

"Me too." Zac agreed, "we should do this again."

"Yeah, I'd like that." I smiled at Zac and caught the twinkle in his eyes. It would be so easy to fall for him and I wanted to, very much. He leaned in and lightly placed his lips on my cheek. I reached up and cupped his cheek.

"I'm going out of town for a few days." Zac said, "leaving tomorrow so can I call you when I'm back?"

"Yes, I'll be around! Probably tied to my desk chasing another pound!"

"I'll come and save you."

"That would be nice." I replied, smiling, feeling my stomach flip a little. "Have a safe trip. Going anywhere nice?"

"I could tell you, but then I'd have to kill you!" Zac grinned.

"Oh, that old chestnut! Be safe, wherever it is you're going." I placed my oyster card down on the pad and the barrier swung open. "I really did have a nice evening, Zac."

"Me too."

I walked across the station to the escalators and turned to wave at Zac. He was already talking on his phone and didn't see me, but I kept my eyes on him as the stairs took me down. He had such a handsome face, strong jawed with crinkles around his eyes and a full mouth. I imagined his body to be strong, defined and battle worn. I wondered if he'd any bullet scars or similar that he wore wearily. It must be a hard job, facing death at every turn, having to take lives when necessary. It took a certain type of person to do that, to sacrifice so much to keep the country safe, that I felt a faint pull. Maybe what I needed after all, was a hero.

I turned slowly around and looked directly into the flashing brown eyes of Lucien. Before I could catch my breath, the escalator jolted and I grabbed onto the handrail in shock. When I looked back up, Lucien had gone.

I shared a carriage with a couple of giggling women talking about a date. I listened to them, mainly to keep my mind from wondering what Lucien had been doing there. Why had he come back into my life now, when things were almost normal, and I was ready to live again? Had he come along to shatter it all and show me that everything I hoped for was just a pipe dream?

He'd made his choice. My broken heart was testament to that, but he'd called for me, and I went. I should not have gone. I should have left him well alone and I certainly should not have gone back again because seeing him the evening before was a huge mistake. It had made everything worse. It was bad enough that he haunted my dreams but now he was all I could think about whilst awake. I longed to touch him, to feel his satin skin under my fingers, I wanted to feel his lips on mine again, the feel of his hands on my body. He had once made me feel so alive that the absence of him had sent my body into a hibernation that I wasn't sure it would wake up from.

It was all such a mess again and I had no idea what to do next. How could I ever be with Zac when I ran to Lucien the moment he called? Seeing Lucien at the station, which wasn't a coincidence because he didn't ever use public transport, had thrown me further to the wolves. What did he want from me?

I got off the tube and walked home. My head hurt a little from two days of alcohol consumption, after six months of abstaining during my social isolation. It didn't help that Lucien was pounding around inside my mind like a washing machine on spin. I longed for quiet and for sleep to come easily. I didn't want to go to bed thinking of Lucien and I didn't want to wake up crying for him. The wounds were raw. Seeing him had torn the edges and it would be even harder to close them up.

I wanted to cry. Properly cry. Curl up on the floor and howl like an injured animal until all the pain went away. Fuck, it was such a mess.

Perhaps I needed a holiday. I'd earned it. I had enough money, I didn't ever go anywhere to spend my wages, so maybe that was the answer. Actually, I laughed mirthlessly to myself, I had no idea what the answer was. Perhaps I would heal eventually. One day, I could move forward and forget that there had ever been someone called Lucien in my life. Perhaps he would go back under whatever rock he had crawled out from and leave me alone.

The flat was empty when I got home and I longed for the loud, messy company of Xander. He was at home so infrequently it felt as though I lived by myself and the loneliness hit me right between the eyes.

I pulled out my phone and dialled a number. A sleepy voice answered, and I said, "hi Anna, it's me."

"Alice, is everything alright?" She asked sluggishly. "Has something happened?"

I bit down hard on my lip and tasted blood. "No, not really. I got home from a night out and Xander isn't here...suddenly I feel really alone."

"Do you want me to come over?" I heard her mumble to someone, and I realised how much I'd lost track of her life. She was in bed with someone and I had no idea who.

"No, it's fine Anna, you have someone there." Tears began to roll silently down my face. "I just wanted to hear a friendly voice." I wiped my face with my sleeve. "I've been shut away working for so long that I've just realised how lonely I feel. I'm sorry I woke you, forget I called, I'm fine, really, just having a wobble. Go back to sleep."

"Are you sure? I can come over to you? I don't mind, Alice, that's what friends are for."

"No, no, it's fine. Stay home. I'll ring you tomorrow. I'm sorry I woke you up."

"I don't want you to be on your own. I'll come over. I can be there in thirty minutes." The voice beside her said something and Anna said, "Make it twenty minutes because I can have a lift."

"No Anna, please stay where you are, really, I'll be fine. I feel better now that I've spoken to you. You stay with your man and you can tell me all about it during daylight hours!" I laughed but it sounded false. "Maybe we could have lunch or something tomorrow?"

"Yeah, I'd like that Alice. Lots to tell you."

"Night Anna."

"Night Alice, love you."

"Love you." I pressed the call end button and threw my phone down on the sofa. Crossing to my little kitchen I opened the fridge and found a bottle of opened wine. I was unsure how long it'd been open but I sniffed it and it smelt ok, so I emptied it into a clean mug and went back to the lounge.

Kicking off my shoes I put my mug down on the table and went to my bedroom to get undressed and into my pyjamas. I felt so tired. The past six months had been exhausting, throwing my entire life into work had kept me from breaking into pieces but it had only masked the pain, rather like a plaster on a ever-growing tumour. I had thought I could be ready to meet someone new, particularly as that person was Zac, handsome, brave, heroic Zac, but Lucien crashing back

into my life had me questioning everything, except how I felt about him.
 Fuck, I was still in love with Lucien.
 Bastard.

LUCIEN

I felt dreadful as I walked away from the hotel. Angela was the playmate I'd had for the longest and aside from my time with Alice – when I was exclusive - she'd been more-or-less consistent. I suspected she'd had more feelings for me than an agreement allowed for, but I'd always treated her correctly – until now.

I crossed the street to the taxi rank and booked one to take me back to the bar where I'd last seen Alice. As awful as it made me appear, my sole intention was to walk into the bar and...well, after that I had no idea. The visions of knights jousting for the hand of the maiden sprung to mind, and despite the twisted feelings I had about what I was doing, the images did make me smile.

I paid the driver as he pulled up outside the bar and I got out of the car, closing the door behind me. I felt almost nervous. It was an odd feeling, guilt was a feeling I had gotten used to, but nerves were a whole new experience. I was nervous. Alice's beau made me edgy and I didn't like it. I had never lost to a man before, not that I knew of, and I didn't intend to start.

That's up to Alice.
Fuck off.

The bar was empty when I looked in through the window. I checked my watch and it was later than I thought. Shit. I looked around and saw them walking into the underground. I ran across the road to the station, with the masochistic reason of finding out if he was going home with Alice. I could taste the jealousy on my tongue, a bitter, acidic taste that made me feel nauseous. I wasn't one for jealously, I'd never needed to be, I usually got my own way with women, but Alice was not other women, she was different.

I hated him.

I stopped a distance from them. My heart was pounding as I waited for his next move. It felt like a game that only I was aware of, but as I waited, I studied him. He was a similar build to me, younger of course, but the ease in which he held her attention made me think that he had something that I didn't. He made her laugh. I don't think I ever did that, perhaps once, when she commented on the pastries I'd bought for the office, but most of the time, I think I made her sad.

I wrapped my hand around Ottie's address and held it tightly in my palm. The piece of paper that John had given me was tatty and I didn't think it would hold together for much longer. It had become a comfort, something to give me strength, although not the strength I needed to go to her. I longed to. But I couldn't do it on my own.

I followed them into the station, maintaining my distance but close enough that I could see her eyes sparkle as he spoke to her. Perhaps she needed someone like him, someone without the baggage that I carried. She deserved someone to make her laugh, all I brought her was pain.

Alice was enjoying his company, but she didn't have that look on her face. There was still hope. She'd proved it yesterday when she had come to see me, checking, I think, that I hadn't ended up like she'd found me once before. I wanted to shout at him that she was mine, but I lost the right to do that when I left her in Paris.

Time was supposed to have numbed the feelings I had for Alice. I was never supposed to have had feelings for anyone again, that why I only fucked women once, maybe twice, and had agreements with willing participants who knew the rules. I didn't ever have relationships. I broke people. I destroyed happiness. It was far better to keep things simple.

Everything had been simple until the day that Alice Addison walked into my office and back chatted me. I should have fired her, should have had her escorted out of the building and out of the way before I could ever have enticed her back to my apartment. Now, I had no one to take the pain away, there were no agreements, no one willing to just fuck. I'd disposed of all of them, the toys and that part of my life. Now there was only the raw and brutal realisation that I would have to face up to my shit and it may be too late to make it up to Alice.

I waited a moment too long.

She saw me in the station and her face flickered between shock, dismay and fleetingly, there was hope. The escalator seemed to jerk, and I watched her grab the rail to stop herself falling. As soon as she took her eyes from mine, I left the station and called for a taxi.

***

"What the fuck do you want?" Alice raged, pale liquid from the mug she held in her hand slopped onto the floor. She didn't appear to notice as she stood glaring at me. "You have a fucking nerve, Lucien."

"That's a friendly welcome." I said lightly. Alice was wearing cotton pyjamas that seemed to mould around her breasts tantalisingly and I felt my cock twitch.

"Why would it be friendly? You're not fucking welcome here. I don't ever want to see you again."

"Are you sure?" I hadn't meant to toy with her, but it was the Lucien she knew, and I didn't know how to be anyone else. The bold, brash, confident Lucien was the role I had played for a decade and was a habit I wore like a comfort blanket. I pulled my hand from my pocket, careful to keep the paper from falling out.

"Extremely." She took a drink from the mug and from the flush on her cheeks I guessed it was alcohol.

I moved closer to her. She still had the soft, floral scent that was both a torment and a drug, that seemed to hold me in a haze of desire, need and a desperate want. I don't think she had any idea as to how mouth-watering she was, particularly standing in her doorway, face scrubbed clean of the day, the mug of wine, I assumed, gripped tightly in her smooth, soft hand.

Alice took a step backwards and looked wary. "Why did you come here, Lucien. Why were you at the station? Are you following me like a weird stalker?"

I smothered a grin. It wasn't the first time she'd called me that and where Alice was concerned, a stalker was probably the right description. She looked at me so fiercely that I wanted to laugh.

"You know me Alice. Weird in general." I shrugged. "Are you going to invite me in?"

"No fucking way."

"Now, now that's not very polite."

"Lucien." She said slowly, as though savouring the syllables. "I don't have to be polite. I don't have to have anything to do with you. You are a liability and no good for me. I don't want you here because you are a complete wanker and I cannot be arsed with your alpha male stalker shit. I've moved on. You have no impact on my life anymore." She visibly shook as she spoke and but never once did Alice look at me.

Because she was lying.

ALICE

Why, oh why, oh why, oh why, did I open the door? Who was I expecting to be on my doorstep at such a late hour? Maybe I was hoping for Zac, instead I opened the door to face the devil and yet, I wasn't surprised it was Lucien. It was inevitable that he would eventually come. Why else would he have been at the underground station if not to further torment me? Lucien knew how to play me, how to get my attention, how to win at the sick games he so enjoyed. I was nothing more than a pawn, a mouse for a warped cat to tease before moving in for the kill.

I couldn't look at Lucien. The sheer closeness to him and to the citrus scent that filled my lungs, was a torture that I would never be able to explain. He had to go because I would weaken and there was no way that I was going to let him in through the front door despite the volume at which my body was calling for his. My breasts strained at the soft fabric of my pyjamas in a way they'd not for months. The proximity to him was awakening the drum beat deep within, the drum that had be silenced for so long and I loathed my body for it

It was a physical pain, the maddening pull to him and I longed to slam the door in his face. I took a step backwards just as Lucien moved towards me.

"Alice…"

"Don't Lucien, don't say anything. Don't do anything. Please just go home." My voice came out in barely a whisper. I couldn't look at him as he took another, smaller, step closer.

"You don't mean that Alice."

I nodded and bit down hard on my lip. "I do. I really do. Once, maybe, you would have gotten away with anything, now, well, I've changed. You can't be here. You can't do this anymore. You can't call me every time some supposed crisis happens. I won't be there again, Lucien. I can't be. You're not good for me. Please go home."

"No."

Before I'd even taken another breath, Lucien had his arms around me, and his demanding mouth was finding mine. I melted into the kiss, the kiss I'd longed for, dreamt about, and craved beyond all reason. I wanted to push him off and lock the door, instead I gave in and kissed him back.

"Alice," he groaned against my mouth, his cock hard against my hip. "Alice."

"Get off me." I groaned weakly. I was losing control of my senses the longer he held me, but I feared how the rejection would hurt if he did let me go.

"Are you sure?" He whispered. "Are you sure you want me to get off?" He stroked my neck and teased the collar of my pyjamas, following the path of his fingertips with his lips. I closed my eyes.

"Yes, I'm sure."

"Use the safe word, Alice."

I wanted to. I wanted to shout *red* at the top of my lungs, for the whole world to hear, like Lucien did in Paris, but I couldn't utter the word. I didn't want him to get off, all my protestations were false, and he knew it. Lucien wouldn't be asking for the safe word if he believed what I was saying. Zac was forgotten as I leaned against Lucien, feeling the singe of nerves each time his mouth touched my skin.

"Well?" He challenged me huskily. "Shall I stop? Are you going to safe-word me?"

His cock twitched against my hip and I felt the heat in my pussy. Even if I'd wanted to safe word him, my body was demanding his and I couldn't utter the word. I felt Lucien's smile against the hollow of my throat, and I gave into my fate.

He kissed my neck and moved up to lightly run his soft tongue along my jaw. There was a gasp, me I supposed, as he lightly nipped the skin, moving to my mouth which fell open as his lips met mine.

Without taking his lips from mine, Lucien popped open the buttons of my pyjama top and ran his hands down my naked body. His palms were soft and warm as he stroked my breasts and my stomach before his touch became firmer, rougher and exactly what I needed. Desire flooded my senses as he cupped my breasts, tugging on my nipples until they were as hard as peanuts. He said nothing as he kissed me with an urgency that matched my own. I needed him. My pussy released its silky juice the longer he held me in his embrace.

"Are you wet for me?" He asked huskily against my lips.

"No." It sounded like a lie, ringing as loudly as a church bell. I didn't want to give him the satisfaction of knowing he'd achieved what he came here for but I couldn't ask him to stop because the words would not come.

"You're a bad liar, Alice." Lucien pushed me into the flat and closed the door with his foot. Once inside, he freed my body from my pyjamas and stood back, appraising me. "I know you want me"

"No, Lucien, I don't." My voice was weak, and his smile spread across his face. Of course, I wanted him, I could see myself reflected in his hooded eyes and my desire was shimmering across my skin. My body was ripe, open, quivering with an orgasm that was already beginning to build. My hunger for Lucien had not passed during the past six months and he knew it.

"Liar." Lucien said, his voice low and gravelly. "Your body gives you away, Alice. It always does. You want me as much as I want you." He gestured down to his groin where his cock was straining against his trousers. "See. I can't lie…"

"Go home, Lucien." I said croaking through dry lips. "Please, go home."

"As I said, Alice, you need to safe word me…"

"Bastard."

He shrugged. "So, they say."

There was a pause and a flash of pain crossed Lucien's face. It was gone as quickly as it had arrived and he moved towards me, the predator to the prey. That we would have sex was inevitable, a twist in my stars, or something, but as he took another step closer to me, I realised I could take something from him.

I could take control.

I stepped backwards and twisted my hair up, running my fingertips along my lips, which fell open at my touch. Slowly, I stroked the soft skin along my collar bone before trailing them down to my heavy breasts. They were high, swollen and burnt under my touch. I was so greedy for the orgasm, yet I touched myself slowly, savouring the feeling of my body ripening. My thumb and forefinger teased my nipples and they hardened until it was almost painful. Lucien took an audible breath in and I opened my legs. I couldn't hide what my body was doing, so I used it.

"Do you like watching?" I asked him huskily, stroking my breasts. "Do you want these?" I cupped my breasts, holding them up as though an offering to the Gods. "Do you want to taste them?" I moved towards him and stood in front of him. Lucien bent his head and took my nipple in his mouth, pulling on it with his lips. I gasped. It felt so good. I stayed still as he took my breasts into his hands and suckled me, one nipple them the other, pulling on them with his teeth. I felt the pull in my pussy and the tightening of my wet channel. The throbbing within because unbearable so I began to stroke myself, my fingers soaked in the silky juice. Lucien's mouth became more insistent, and he clung to me as he pulled at my breasts with his mouth.

I would never tire of him.

My fingers stroked my clitoris as wave after wave of delicious heat flooded my body, it felt so good, so good to have Lucien suckling me, to feel the wetness between my legs and the burn of desire. I reached out with my other hand and unbuttoned his fly, taking the gargantuan cock into my palm. The skin around the hardness was like velvet and I gripped him tightly, moving my hand back and forth until he was gasping.

"Suck me." Lucien begged. "Suck my cock, please Alice, suck me."

I knelt down. His cock was twitching, and the droplets of juice pooled in the end. I licked them off, savouring the salty taste and wrapped my mouth around the engorged head. Fuck me, he tasted good. So good. With a thirst for him, I sucked and licked, taking every droplet, cupping his sac with my hand and squeezing as I took his length down into my throat. My pussy ached as Lucien fucked my mouth until the final gasps and the explosion of cum. I licked every drop, keeping him hard in my mouth until there was nothing left.

"Alice." He whispered gripping my hair. "I've missed you."

Lucien pushed me down onto the sofa, tipping the paraphernalia onto the floor and lying above me, he looked at me as though he was seeing me for the first time. Softly he lowered his mouth to mine and gave me a kiss that seemed filled with an indescribable emotion and I realised that he had missed me like I missed him and for a moment the stars collided.

For a moment it was all real.

Lucien softly stroked my body, looking as though he was seeing me for the first time, his attention melted my insides until I was a shimmering ball of light. I was exactly where I wanted to be, Lucien was being exactly who I wanted him to be and there was a magic in the air. We moved together, slowly, as Lucien slid his cock into me and I held him to me tightly, my legs around his waist and my arms around his shoulders.

We were one, for that perfect moment, two souls with a powerful longing for one another, and my orgasm, when I gave into it, was like none I'd ever experienced, it was a connection to something so deep, so primal, so breath-taking that the world began to sway in front of my eyes, and I went with it, letting the blackness take me. I heard Lucien calling my name.

LUCIEN

"You had me worried for a moment." I said handing Alice a bar of chocolate I'd found buried in the fridge. It looked questionable, a little furry and an shade of off-white, but there wasn't anything else that would give Alice a sugar rush. "I thought I'd killed you!"

"Death by orgasm." Alice smiled, weakly. She rubbed the top of her head and a flash of pain crossed her face. "I'm not sure my mum would want that on the certificate." She touched her forehead and winced. "Do I have an egg?"

"A very red egg," I said breaking the chocolate for her and handing her a square. "I've no idea if this will work, the internet said it would, a sugar rush or something…"

"I think I've had enough rush for this evening." She said taking it from me. "Thank you." Alice put the square in her mouth and pulled a face. "Do we not have any dairy milk anywhere, this is Xander's revolting healthy chocolate!"

I looked down at the packet. "You have nothing. It's no wonder you look skinny, your fridge is completely empty, what do you live off?" I nodded at the chocolate, "you do realise that it is ninety percent Costa Rican beans, that's the Lamborghini of chocolate."

"Well…fuck."

"Again?" I grinned and broke off another piece of the chocolate for myself. It tasted like shit. I took a tissue from the box on the side table and spat it out. "Do you want me to go and get you some dairy milk?"

"If you go, will you come back?"

I don't think she meant to ask as Alice's cheeks flushed a dark shade of red that looked macabre against the grey of her post-faint face. I reached out and cupped her cheek in my hand, lightly brushing my thumb over the raised bone of her cheek. Alice looked as though she wished she could take the words back and I felt an ache in the centre of my chest. I'd massively fucked up with her and there was no way that I could ever do that to her again.

"Yes," I said softly. "Yes, I will be back."

Alice smiled and the flush in her face lightened. "Good."

My phone beeped from the sofa behind her and she reached back for it. I watched her glance down at the screen and the light redness faded to a sickly yellow colour. I felt my stomach hit the floor. Shit, what was on the screen?

"Alice?" I asked in a thick voice, holding my hand out for my phone. She stared down at it and I swallowed a concrete lump before saying her name again. Alice was so still, like a statue, staring unblinkingly at the writing on the phone screen.

"Alice?" I repeated again, crouching down in front of her. I wanted to take the phone, but Alice's reaction was so unnerving, I didn't dare do anything other than wait for her to speak. When she did her voice was hollow and empty.

"It seems that you are needed, *Sir*..." There was so much emphasis on the *sir* that I could only imagine what the message said. I took a breath but I couldn't get any air in my lungs. One by one my ribs felt as though they were fracturing, and the shards punctured my chest until I saw spots in front of my eyes.

The text could have been from any number of women, women who had no idea that I was no longer on the scene. I'd only told Angela, it had never occurred to me that I should have closed play with the others. It had never crossed my mind that the preferences I'd had for a while would explode all over everything I needed to have in my life. Alice looked like she had been shot.

"It's not what you think." Even to me it sounded feeble, a pathetic attempt to brush it under the carpet.

"Isn't it?" Alice wrapped the blanket from the back of the sofa around her naked self. "I suppose you're going to tell me that there is a simple explanation? That someone isn't waiting for you to do kinky shit to them?" Alice looked sickened and tightened her grip on the blanket. "I am such a fool." She whispered, her voice breaking. "Such a fool."

"No Alice, no you're not."

"No?" She raised stricken eyes up to mine. The red bump on her forehead looked all the more vivid against the pale skin of her face. "You were not going to come back, were you? You were moving onto the next sad cow who needed fucking or whatever it was you had planned for them. You got what you wanted here didn't you, so it has made it easy to leave. You won Lucien. You got to me, like you knew you would, because you wanted to win above everything else. You have no more feelings for me than the woman in that message. We are nothing to you but games to play. Go to her. I don't want you here. I was doing great before you came back into my life and there is no room for you now."

"Alice…you're wrong."

"I said for you to go." She hissed. "I hate you Lucien. You are despicable. I hate how much you make me hate myself. I was getting somewhere finally, at work and in my personal life and now you've fucked it all up." Alice pulled herself up from the sofa and making sure her beautiful body was completely covered she walked to the front door and opened it. "You have to go. I can't be near you, you make me sick. You are nothing but an egomaniac arsehole and I do not want you here any longer."

I stood up from the crouched position and put my phone in my pocket. There was so much to tell her, so much to say, an entire past to explain but the words would not come. Silently, I walked from the room and onto the landing. I turned to speak to her, to reach out and tell her everything, tell her all my shit, all the demons, everything, but the door slammed behind me and Alice was gone.

ALICE

It was the weekend from hell. Xander didn't come home and Anna was busy, so I lay on the sofa alternating between crying hysterically and the having complete absence of feeling. It was a strange numbness, as though my mind was shutting down to escape the gripping, slicing pain, but my mind couldn't keep the agony locked away for long, and that's when the anguish came.

What had I been thinking? Why did I let Lucien in? Had I not learnt anything from last time? Self-loathing churned my stomach, sending acid raging through my insides until everything was charred and useless. I had just about survived the last six months, I'd just about kept myself from crumbling into dust, but I wasn't sure I could survive this.

I was nothing to Lucien except for being someone over whom he could exert his power. I should have never let him in.

Zac had text me a couple of times, but I'd not yet replied. The guilt I was feeling about him was eating away at me and I wondered how I had ended up being the kind of person that I disliked – a liar and a cheat. It was, perhaps, slightly over dramatic, but I was feeling far from rational. I was feeling utterly hateful towards the world and all because I had, perhaps, cheated on the one person who may be able give me what I was so desperate for – love.

I wasn't looking for the sappy Disney-esque happy-ever-after romance, but I'd always longed for the one true love, because at the ripe old age of twenty-eight I'd never once found it. The first love had passed me by - I was always the friend, the one to confide in or the third wheel. There was never anyone who looked at me the way the boys looked at my friends with puppy dog eyes. I was just 'good old Alice' and it wasn't until university that anyone appeared to fancy me.

I got lost in romance stories and cheap pints of beer, the occasional one-night stand while harbouring endless crushes that no one ever knew about. My sister was the complete opposite to me, she was out there, always in love with someone new and after I moved to London, Anna took over from my sister, and my job was to pick up her pieces each time the blissful, perfect romance went wrong.

I assumed there was something wrong with me and that I didn't have the 'love gene.' I was sure that I was just destined to be the 'friend' or worse, the pitied single friend who got dragged on various dates my friends went on as a back-up if it went wrong. Even worse than that, often I was fixed up with the date's best friend, a man who was always single for a reason! Yet somehow, I'd fallen in love with Lucien, the handsome, damaged protagonist in my pathetic life story, but far from being a fairy tale, it had become the stuff of nightmares.

I wanted to reply to Zac but the guilt I felt made me feel so sick that I just lay on the sofa in manky old pyjamas, slowly becoming more and more desolate. Every time I closed my eyes, I saw the text message, the delinquent sex acts described by the woman who was asking for it, and I wondered over and over how I could have ever got mixed up in any of that.

I enjoyed kinky sex, it was exciting, sordid, warped and gave me such intense orgasms that I had wanted more and more. But it wasn't the biggest part of me and at that moment I could never envisage doing any of it again. The voice in my head whispered that what I wanted was for Lucien to love me. I wanted to shut up the inner-me, tell her to let it go, he would never feel for me the way I felt for him, and no amount of hoping would change that.

In the end, I covered my pyjamas with a long coat, pulled on my shoes and went to the corner shop for over-priced wine and a family sized bag of crisps.

I don't remember going to bed.

***

"I did something." Saffron said, handing me a coffee and looking sheepish. "I did something, and I think you're going to go completely nuts."

I was so tired that my eyeballs felt like they had been boiled in acid. I yawned widely, my jaw popping, as I flopped down into my chair.

"Are you alright, Alice?" She asked, concern creeping into her voice. "Shall I save my bombshell for later? Should I ask you about Zac instead? I noticed you two snuck off together on Friday. That's exciting!"

Friday seemed a lifetime ago. It was hard to remember what happened an hour ago and instead of answering Saffron, I took a sip of the coffee and the heat of the liquid scalded my tongue. "Ouch, bugger that's hot."

"Sorry." Saffron mumbled, "I should have said that I'd literally jut made it. You looked knackered...should I ask?"

"I didn't sleep well..." That was the understatement of the century. I'd barely slept all weekend and black spots of dizziness kept creeping across my eyes. I wondered if I'd done some damage when I passed out and fell. It was hard to know. Spending the weekend on the sofa made me so lethargic that I didn't know if I had concussion or just the effects of being stagnant. "So, what's the bombshell and do I really want to know?" I asked blowing on the coffee. There wasn't enough coffee in the world to shift my exhaustion. Saffron shifted from foot to foot. "Come on Saff, it can't be that bad!"

"I think it can."

"You're not leaving?"

"No!" Saffron exclaimed. "Well, you may make me leave..."

"What have you done?"

Saffron looked terrified. "I entered you into the Outstanding Young Entrepreneur competition"

"What?" I choked, feeling the blood drain from my face. "What? What did you do?"

"I'm sorry." Saffron's face crumpled and she looked close to tears. "I had a reminder email about it last week, and I thought it would be a great opportunity for you to be considered. You've worked so hard, it would be a real coup for you and huge recognition for what you've done with your business. You are a young entrepreneur, Alice, I thought everyone should know…I'm sorry, I shouldn't have done it without asking you, but I thought you'd say no, and really, you deserve to win it."

I wanted to reassure Saffron that she had done the right thing by entering me into the competition, but Lucien was on the board of the Directors of London Commerce, the city's most successful company owners who voted for the winners and rather than feel proud of Saffron's belief in me, I wanted to vomit. I was convinced that someone somewhere was out to get me, that I'd offended whomever it was so immensely in my last life, that this life was all about the pay back.

Saffron was nervously biting her nails and looking as though she would cry at any moment. I didn't want to drag her down to my level of bleakness, so I attempted a smile and swallowed the nausea.

"Thank you." I proffered through dry lips. "Thank you for believing in me and for putting the entry in. I would have never put myself forward, it's a huge competition and you're right, it could be massive for us to be considered, even if we don't stand a chance at winning. Sorry my initial reaction wasn't what you'd hoped for, it has been a miserable weekend and I'm a little grumpy."

"Missing Zac?" She asked cheekily. I flushed. If only life was as simple as that. Saffron changed the conversation. "I've been looking at the competition for the prize in your category and there isn't anyone who really stands out, you're definitely in with a good chance of winning. What would you do with the prize money? It's twenty grand!"

"Is it really?" I asked shocked. "Twenty thousand pounds?"

"Yes!" Saffron said, jigging up and down on the balls of her feet. "Twenty big ones. I know what I'd do…"

"What would you do?" I asked, raising the coffee to my lips.

"I'd go to New York and stay in the hotel I saw on tv. It's so chic, with a rooftop pool and a butler for each suite and I'd fly first class and drink champagne, and I'd shop in every store on Fifth Avenue, like a celebrity. It would be amazing." Saffron had a far away look in her eyes. It did sound bliss.

"I tell you what, Saff. If I win, you can have half the money to go to New York with…"

"I couldn't take half, that's madness, think what you could do with it. You could hire someone else to make us coffee, pay Xander back…"

I laughed. "I could! I could hire a skivvy and give Xander the final thousand I owe him, or we could spend it on something that makes us happy and make memories. That is priceless, don't you think? We've certainly worked hard enough for it."

"What would you spend it on?" Saffron asked. "You could come to New York with me!"

"Yeah, New York would be something special, but, actually, thinking about it, I'd go somewhere tropical, and quiet, a hotel near the sea so I could fall asleep to the sounds of the ocean. I feel worn out that a complete break would be so welcome. Perhaps I'd go to the Caribbean, drink rum all day and lie in the sunshine, read a book…"

"It sounds a bit middle aged if I'm honest!" Saffron said grinning. "You're twenty-eight, you should be going to Miami or LA or Aya Napa and party all night with hot, half naked men!" Saffron's eyes widened. "Or somewhere with Zac!"

I flushed. "You don't even know that Zac likes me, Saffron! I could have just been the best option on Friday!"

"Trust me, he likes you!"

It made me feel worse. The hope on her face that I would feel something for her brother added to the sickening feeling in the pit of my stomach.

"Who likes who?" The deep voice asked behind us. Zac walked into our section and grinned. "Hello ladies, gossiping instead of working?"

I felt a warmth flood my cheeks. "Hi Zac."

"You're back!" Saffron squealed, leaping up to give Zac a bear hug. "Where did you go? Did anyone try and shoot you? Did you shoot anyone? Did you save a president or a princess or…"

"Not this time, and as for where I went, I could tell you but then I'd have to kill you!"

"Not that again, you're so dull." Saffron said sitting down. "You have the most exciting job in the world and say nothing about it. Do you have any idea how frustrating that is?"

"Do you have any idea how much I like winding you up?" Zac teased. "It's so easy."

"Piss off Zac. Why are you here bothering us anyway, don't you know we're busy and important?"

Zac looked at us, the open packet of biscuits and numerous discarded coffee cups. "It looks like you are!"

"Looks can be deceiving." I said smiling. "We have been having a team meeting."

"I'm not convinced you two do anything!" Zac teased. "Anyway, I'm back and I wondered about dragging you out for coffee, Alice? If you can squeeze me into your busy day."

"Oh, she's not busy!" Saffron said breezily. "She's all yours."

My heart sank. Saffron meant well and Zac was so handsome I could have looked at him all day but I was bruised and battle scarred from my run in with Lucien and all I really wanted to do was hide from the world, in our cubby hole in a corner of Shoreditch and bury myself under a pile of work to stop me dwelling. Instead, I said, "coffee would be great."

Saffron beamed as I picked up my coat. It was a cold day and the draft coming in through the windows was bitter. I shrugged my arms into my coat and followed Zac out of the building. The Hub was buzzing with noise and the ringing of phones, but I felt distant from it. Tiredness, perhaps, or the loss of my soul to the devil. Yes, that was more like it. I'd paid the ferryman and the price had been far too high.

Zac held the door for me and we walked down the stairs into the biting wind. Winter had taken full effect and the brown leaves, that somehow survived autumn, were whipping by.

"Gosh, it's so cold." I commented through chattering teeth. "It's not supposed to be this cold now!"

"I could bore you with my weather knowledge, or I could warm you up." There was an invitation in his words that increased the guilt I was already feeling. It seemed strange to have cheating weighing on me when Zac and I had only had one kiss and a couple of drinks. His eyes shined as he chatted while we walked along the road. He was easy to be with and so handsome that I kept catching myself staring at him. If he noticed, Zac said nothing, just walked amiably beside me until I stopped, suddenly aware of eyes on me.

Lucien.

Goddamn it.

I pretended I had something in my shoe and dropped to a crouch as I tried to scan the area without being too obvious. My instincts were spot on and standing across the road was Lucien, a small bunch of flowers in his hand. They were nothing like the enormous blooms that arrived on my doorstep only a few short weeks ago, and it tore my heart. Somehow it was far easier to ignore the ostentatious flowers he'd had delivered than a small bouquet of delicate looking blooms.

I longed to run over, smack them around his face and tell him to fuck off and leave me alone forever. Instead, when Zac crouched down beside me, I pulled him into a deep kiss.

It was so wrong of me.

I was a complete bitch to have done that, but the kiss was nice, and soft and made me feel floaty.

When I pulled away, Lucien had gone, and the flowers were in a lamppost bin.

LUCIEN

I was man enough to admit that I deserved that. I would have deserved everything that Alice could throw at me, but the jealousy was so palpable that it was as though I was facing a rage monster. I could barely see through the blur in front of my eyes as Alice kissed him.

I knew she was doing it to piss me off, the intent was in her face when she saw me watching them. She wanted to prove a point and it worked far too well. I couldn't stand there for long, the urge to rip his head off was all too real so I stuffed the flowers I'd bought Alice into a bin and turned back along the road to hail a taxi.

Back in the office I couldn't focus on work. It needed my complete attention because there was too much to do and I'd had my eye off the ball for far too long. It didn't help that Carol was glowering at me from behind her desk which was an irritant I could have done well without. I could see her mentally ticking off the items on my list, like a formidable teacher almost daring me to fail so I put my head down and got on with the tasks in hand.

I was worried. The country was facing recession and if I didn't bring in some more business it would be a tight financial year for the company. The business was all mine, there no investors or board of directors to answer to, but perhaps that aided my complacency. I had no one breathing down my neck and my ineffectual leadership over recent months was showing in the figures. The staff deserved me at my best, they worked hard, and they put up with my questionable management style without too much complaint. There was a lull across the departments, and whether that was down to my recent apathy or the doom and gloom projected by the financial press, I didn't know. It seemed so different when Alice was here.

I reached across my desk for the piece of paper with Ottie's address on it. I had to go. Somehow, I had to find the strength in me to go alone. There was no one who had my back anymore, I'd pushed everyone away over the years and had shit on Alice from a great height. It was she who I wanted by my side, to hold my hand as I faced my demon head on, but I feared I had lost her for good and I had no idea what to do to make amends. Very likely I was far too late, and Mr Perfect had swept her off her feet - only my heart didn't believe that.

Not after Friday.

"Mr Ross?" Carol said coming into my office. She still irked me and everything about her from her steely grey hair to her sensible skirts irritated me. She was excellent at her job so professionally I had nothing to complain about particularly as she was more efficient than any assistant I'd ever had. It didn't stop me longing for the banter, back chat and hot sex that I'd had with Alice. Just thinking about her, naked and wet, so willing to please, got my cock hard.

I shifted in my seat.

I had royally screwed that up. Everything about me was a complete fuck up. Isabelle was right.

"Yes?" I asked thinking the gym would be a good place to burn off the increasing anger I felt towards Alice's beau and the increasing discomfort in my cock.

"You've had a package."

"From?"

Carol turned the package over and read the label. "From the Directors of London Commerce. I am assuming they have the final applicants for you to judge."

"When is the event?" I asked flicking on my calendar.

Carol tapped on a tablet. When she got it, I had no idea, but I'd spent much of the past few months in a haze of whiskey that she could have bought out Harrods on expenses for all I knew. "A week on Friday. I have replied that you will be attending, I assume it hasn't changed?"

"Did I ask you to?" I asked opening my calendar.

"Yes." She snapped. "Obviously you don't remember the conversation?"

"Carol?"

"Yes, Mr Ross?"

"Why do you work here?"

Carol flushed. "You pay me a lot more than I'd get elsewhere."

"Carol?"

She sighed. "Yes?"

"You don't like me very much, do you?"

"It doesn't matter if I do or if I don't."

"Perhaps it matters to me." I said, surprising myself. Carol looked taken aback.

She thought for a moment and then said, "Mr Ross, you can be very charming and there are many on your staff who think highly of you, in one way or another. You run a good ship here, but sometimes I think your ego gets in the way and you can be a bit of an arse!"

It was my turn to look surprised. In the six months Carol had worked for me I'd never once heard her swear out loud, although there were plenty of times that I'd heard her whisper an expletive, usually directed at me, under her breath.

I laughed. "I certainly am that, and you're not the first PA I've had to say something similar."

"I assume you are talking about Alice?"

"Alice?"

"You had me call her. I assumed..." Carol flushed. "Sorry Mr Ross, I spoke out of turn, I must get on."

As quick as a flash she turned on her sensible shoes and was out of the office. I reached for the package she'd given me and opened the envelope. There were considerable applicants for Outstanding Young Entrepreneur but only one drew my attention. Alice.

***

Carol had the courier collect my vote for the award. I'd wanted to vote for Alice, she deserved the success of winning the award, but I knew it would have smacked of nepotism, so I resisted. Then I went to the gym. Work could wait.

Of course, the office 'girls' all followed me down, and the egomaniac in me revelled in their furtive glances and hard nipples. Their blatant attraction towards me was a massive boost to my apparently overinflated ego so I put on a show for them and their responses kicked the demons into touch. Just for a moment until the voices whispered Alice's name and the longing for her sat like a rock in my belly.

I lifted as heavy a weight as my body could cope with and the sweat ran in rivers down my back. They liked it, liked the raw masculinity I expect, but if they really knew about me, they would run a mile.

I worked out until there was no strength left in me and the ache in my cock had dispersed. It didn't quell the urge to fuck, but it took the discomfort away and I actually managed to complete my work for that day. I clearly passed the whatever test Carol had for me, she came in to wish me a good evening and as I watched her retreat from my office, I wondered if she could be this company's saving grace.

When I left the office, Alice was firmly in my head and I found myself outside her flat. The light was on and I could see figures moving behind the curtains. I wondered if it was him, there to make her laugh, make love to her, to touch her body the way she liked it to be touched. Fuck, I felt sick. I could feel the metallic taste of nausea in my mouth and I wanted to throw it all up – my pain, the demons, the past, the present, the cunt I was, I wanted to be rid of it all. There was a demon on my shoulder whispering about a bar, any bar and a woman, any woman, one to submit to my every twisted, fucked up desire.

I gave one last look to the figure in the window and went home alone, to the empty flat where the biggest demon of all lurked waiting for me - loneliness.

Perhaps a cunt like me deserved it. I'd broken everything and everyone, maybe this was my penance. I wrapped my hand around the address in my pocket. "I'm so sorry, Ottie. I whispered, "please forgive me."

ALICE

Xander had finally come home. He had made me jump as he crashed in through the front door with a bunch of corner-shop flowers in garish colours and a bottle. He had, as he explained, come up for air and needed a night alone in his own bed, without the distraction of his hot, naked beau. It made me so happy that he had the great love he'd always wanted, and Hugo was so perfect for Xander that he was almost a gift from the Gods – in fact their relationship was so perfect my envy was the third person in the room.

"Shall I pour the green-eyed monster sitting beside you some champagne too?" Xander asked grinning, holding out a glass of champagne for me. "This didn't come from the corner shop, I'd like to point out!"

"I gathered, although their cheapest wine is probably as expensive. Why the champers Xan? Has your trust fund gone up?"

"Not exactly." He said, flopping down on the sofa beside me.

"So…?" I waited. Xander didn't look at me.

"So, can't I treat my favourite girl to expensive champagne?"

"Xander!" I said sharply. "You never treat me to anything more than cheap plonk and furry chocolate…"

"It wouldn't have been furry if you'd eaten it earlier!" Xander said sighing. "It's expensive chocolate…"

"It was disgusting!" I shuddered. Not only was it disgusting but it made me think of Lucien and I wished I'd not brought the subject up.

"You lack refined tastes, my dear Alice." Xander wriggled up to sitting and half downed his champagne, letting out a loud burp as the bubbles hit his stomach.

"Classy as always!" I commented, taking a sip of mine. It was sharp, cold and fizzy. As lovely as it was for Xander to bring home expensive drinks, I couldn't help wondering if there was something more to his generosity.

"How's work?" He asked, wrapping two hands around the chipped wine glass that housed his drink.

"Really busy and stressful but good." I said, snuggling into him. Xander wrapped his arm around me. "Saffron entered me for Outstanding Young Entrepreneur and the voting is this week. I'll know on Friday if I've been nominated for the award and the actual show is a week Friday. I'm really hoping I've not got further than her application."

"But that's incredible news!" Xander said sounding delighted as he squeezed me. "You absolutely should have entered yourself anyway. Why do you always hide your fabulousness away? I know all about that award, Hugo's dad is on the board and it's a massive deal. Past winners are now sitting on the board of multi-million-pound businesses."

"I don't want a multi-million-pound business, or a board." I protested. "I can barely keep up with the small business and one employee that I have!"

"You think too small." Xander said, draining his drink. "You need to think huge!"

"Maybe. One day, perhaps. Right now, there is Saffron and me and we have more work than is manageable."

"Employ someone else then!" Xander refilled his glass and shifted to look at me. "Do you need more money?"

"Thanks Xan but I've nearly paid you back, I don't want to owe anything else." I kissed his cheek. "You are absolutely the best friend a girl could ask for. Sometimes I wonder how life would have been if we hadn't both been dumped and ended up drunk on a bench together."

"It would have been shit. You're my most beloved and if I was straight…"

"You'd be a huge tart and I would go nowhere near you!" I laughed.

"It's nice to be here." Xander said pulling me back into him. He was warm and smelt all Xander-y. He was my love, my saviour, the hero who picked me up when I fell but I had the sense that this would be the last time we would sit like this as flatmates and I waited for the axe to drop.

"Alice?"

"Hmm?" I replied, curling my legs up under me.

"I have something to say."

There it was. The axe was being sharpened. I felt my stomach contract.

"Ok." My voice sounded a little choked and I took a drink of the champagne to soothe it.

Xander cleared his throat and pulled me tighter into him. "Alice, Hugo and I…" He paused and my throat closed over. "Well, we want to live together and…" Xander kissed my head and I closed my eyes tightly against the stinging. "He asked me to marry him and I said yes."

"Oh my God!" I shrieked, slopping champagne all over the two of us. "Oh my God, that is epic news! Epic. I am so pleased." The tears began to roll down my cheeks as my heart ached for me but rejoiced for Xander. He took my tears as those of happiness and threw his arms around me. Somehow, we ended up jumping around the room and whooping until the woman in the flat below banged on the ceiling. We burst out laughing and the ache in my heart was pushed away by the joy.

"I'm so delighted Xander, I am going to burst!" I wrapped my arms around him and took big, deep breaths in.

"I'm so pleased you're pleased." Xander said, his voice breaking. "Because until I met Hugo, you were the love of my life, my very best friend, the reason I could feel proud of who I really was. You did this, Alice, you gave me the strength to finally be me and you will never know what that means. I can never explain to you how much your faith and love and belief in me has lit some very dark times. I never thought I would be accepted by anyone or that I would find true love, the proper kind, with someone who really loves me back. It was all because of you."

I couldn't speak. The lump in my throat from Xander's words, from his love for me and the indestructible bond we had was constricting my airway. For a moment we just held each other, and I knew it would be the last time as flatmates, that moments like this would be part of our history and the future relationship was going to be something so different.

"Also…" Xander whispered, "as my very best friend it does mean that you have to be my best woman!"

"Your what?" I asked.

"My best woman, like a best man but, you know, the woman version."

"Well…shit!"

Xander laughed, "that's what I told Hugo you'd say!"

***

Xander was drunkenly snoring on the sofa as I let myself out of the flat. It was pretty late and the rain was coming down, but I put up my hood and turned along the pavement. I had no real idea where I was headed but I needed to be outside, in the air. It was a strange thing to do on a miserable Sunday night, but I felt as though everything was changing faster than I could keep up with and I needed to be away from the flat.

My phone beeped in my pocket and as I pulled it out, watching as the rain drops fought for space on the screen, and saw a message from Zac.

Hi, it read. *Just checking you're alive?*

I felt gripping guilt. Shit. What was I doing? I'd ignored Zac's messages all weekend when I should have just treated him better. Who was I? I shoved the phone back in my pocket until I reached the covering of the underground station.

Hi. I replied. *Sorry I've not replied. Been a crazy weekend! How are you? Are you back?*

She speaks!!! I'm ok thanks, away still, hoping to be back on Wednesday, this job is a little on the dull side! How's life in London?

London is very wet and miserable tonight. Hope you're somewhere with sunshine?

It's too bloody hot!

Aha so...hmmm...where do I think you are? Sunning yourself in Dubai? Lolling on a beach in Ibiza...am I close?

Very cold!

Bugger – ok, so not those places, perhaps you're in Australia?

I wish!

The Sahara?

That would be a lot more fun than where I am!

I shall think harder!

So, Zac asked. *What are you doing on this rainy Sunday?*

I'm out for a walk! Random, I know! Xander brought champagne over, I'm sobering up!

For someone who claims to have no life, you're doing pretty well!

For the moment! The harsh reality of work beckons!

I hope my sister is behaving?

Your sister is my Girl Friday and every other day!

Bugger, Duty calls...Can I see you when I'm back?

Yes, I replied. *I'd like that.*

Cool! X

I put my phone back into my pocket and stood under the awning looking at the rain. It seemed to fall in perfectly straight lines, silver against the white lights of the cars that passed. I was so happy for Xander, marrying his true love but the rain seemed to mirror the internal battle I had, happiness and the darkest sadness. No more Xander in my little flat with his loud, messy wonderfulness. It was going to feel so empty with him gone.

I waited for a break in the rain and walked along to the late-night café. I used to go there on the way home from a drunken night out for one of their mammoth fry-ups but that had long stopped. I didn't even know if it remained open, but I walked towards it anyway, in search of hot coffee to sober me up. I don't know why I thought of there. I had plenty of coffee in the cupboards. I needed it to keep me going because something had to get me out of bed every day. The endless nights of tears and bad dreams had taken their toll a long time ago and coffee was the only thing that kept the exhaustion at bay. I didn't make it to the café, because the black car pulled up alongside me.

"Alice. What are you doing, it's too late to be out?"

"Fuck off, Lucien."

"Alice, please, get in the car, it's raining and there are a lot of weird people around..."

"Says the weirdest one of all." I shoved my hands in my pockets and kept walking. Lucien followed slowly alongside the kerb.

"Let me at least take you home. It's not safe to be out at this time of night. This is London..."

"I am very aware that this is London, Lucien but I would rather take my chances on the street than get in the car with you. Why are you here anyway? You live across town. Why can't you just go the fuck away?"

"Because I don't want to." Almost before I could take a breath, he was beside me, the car idling at the kerb. "I have things to say to you Alice and you have to listen." Lucien sounded almost desperate and it took every ounce of strength I had to keep my resolve. I couldn't listen, I couldn't have anything to do with him as much as I longed to fling myself into his arms and kiss him.

"No, I don't." I shot back. "I am done with you. When are you going to realise that? I did my penance for all the lies I told during our…what did you call it? An agreement? I've paid for that, Lucien, I paid for that with my pride and my sanity and my sentence was up the day I had to rescue you from too much whiskey in a disgusting dive bar. So, I will not listen, and I won't stand here for another second with you."

"Alice…"

"No." I said, my voice loud on the silent street. "NO. You can't keep doing this, you can't keep showing up and expecting me to jump however high you tell me too. I'm not the same Alice that I was, I changed the moment you left me in Paris. Please, just leave me to live my life, let me finish fixing…" I stopped abruptly before I could say anymore.

"Fixing what, Alice?" Lucien asked, his voice soft.

"It doesn't matter." I shook my head and shrugged. "It's all history. Good night, Lucien."

Lucien reached for my hand and captured it inside of his warm palm before I could drag it away from him. The feeling of his skin on mine tingled the nerves in my hand and sent light through my veins.

"Let me go." I said weakly.

"Not this time."

"It's too late, Lucien. There is someone else in my life."

"It didn't appear that way on Friday." He said smoothly.

"Friday was a monumental mistake, and one I will never, ever repeat, so please let me go."

Lucien moved closer to me, close enough that I could smell his scent. I closed my eyes, willing the rain to wash this evening away, but when I opened them, Lucien was watching me, a knowing smile on his lips.

"Don't look at me like that." I seethed, pulling my hand sharply from his. My palm went cold, and I rubbed it to get the warmth back. "Don't stand in my space and don't…"

"What's the matter Alice? Do I make you nervous?"

"Nervous? You! Ha!" I said with faux humour, removing a strand of wet hair from my face. "You'd be surprised how little you make me feel anything."

"You're such a liar, Alice." Lucien said softly, moving closer again. I could feel the warmth of his body from the mere inches we were apart and that, coupled with the scent of him, was too much for me to bear. I took a step backwards, hoping for enough distance to assemble my jumbled thoughts. Lucien grinned and I moved again, feeling the wall of the underground smacking into my back.

There was nowhere to go.

He had me trapped.

LUCIEN

From the way Alice was trembling I knew that everything she was throwing at me was a lie designed to make me leave. It didn't work. I was so close I could smell her floral perfume and it was driving me crazy. Every time I moved closer to her, it stirred something completely primal in me, a desire so strong I wanted to fuck her right there on the street.

I know she wanted me too. Every few seconds her tongue would dart out and moisten her lips and the quiet clearing of her throat told me that I was getting to her. Just like she was getting to me.

My cock was twitching and hardening in my trousers and I deliberately taunted Alice with it, moving nearer still so that she could feel what she was doing to me. Slowly I rubbed myself against her and her mouth fell open, a barely-audible sigh escaping from her lips.

"You want me, don't you?" I murmured into her ear.

Alice stiffened and then said, "no."

"Liar." I breathed, nipping her earlobe. Alice gasped and tensed.

"Get off me Lucien."

"I'm not on you, Alice. Not yet anyway, but I think you know you'll be coming home with me."

"You must be fucking joking." Alice snapped, seeming to come out of the trance she had been in. I gripped her wrists in my hands and help them up against the wall. "Get off me Lucien." Her voice weakened and she didn't try to move.

"You don't want me? Use the safe word and I'll let you go."

"You are a complete bastard." Alice groaned as I leaned my body against hers. She could feel my cock, straining against my trousers, pressing into her stomach. It was so hard it hurt, and I longed to bend her over and slide into her, right there in the street. I didn't want to wait, Alice did things to me, made me so completely animalistic that I had no cares about being seen. I just wanted to feel her hot, wet pussy gripping my cock as she came.

"Please get off me." She whispered. Alice had her eyes closed and she seemed to be breathing more deeply that I would have expected, as though she was trying to calm herself or ebb the flow of longing that she was obviously battling. I hadn't planned for this, I hadn't planned for the public face of me to take over, I'd wanted to tell her everything and open up completely but instead the hunger took over and the Lucien she knew, exploded outwards.

"Alice..."

"Lucien, please...don't do this." I was horrified to see a tear roll down her face. Alice bit down on her lip and squeezed her eyes shut. "I can't go there with you again; you took everything from me when you left."

"I'm sorry, Alice." I said desolately, letting her hands go and moving back from her. My cock deflated as her words sunk in. What the fuck was I doing, dragging her back into my mess? Alice didn't deserve that, she was a better person than I could ever be. "I'm sorry I came back into your life. I meant to stay away. You deserve better than the shit I have to offer."

"All you can offer are agreements, Lucien." She said, wrapping her arms around herself and looking down to the puddle of rain water under her feet. "That text message you got from one of your many fuck-pieces proved that. I don't want that. What makes me feel sick to my stomach is that there were other agreements at the same time as me. I was so blind not to have seen it. I was nothing to you. NOTHING."

She shouted and gave me a shove that pushed me backwards into the rain.

"That's not true." I protested. "There were no others when you and I..."

"You and I? There wasn't a you and I, Lucien, there were only sordid kinky fucks. I was nothing." Alice laughed harshly, the sound was like nails down a blackboard and I gritted my teeth.

"You were not *nothing*."

"I was." She cried, tears cascading down her face. I wanted to comfort her, but it was her rejection I feared most. "I must have been. It was too easy for you to leave."

"Alice..." It was my chance to explain, to tell her everything. I wanted to make amends, let her see the real Lucien but Alice moved suddenly and placed her hands on my cheeks, pulling my face to hers. She kissed me frantically, her hands moved from my cheeks to my hair, holding me close to her. I could feel her tears on my skin and I longed to make it better for her. The truth would set me free, but it would pull her into the dark world I'd been inhabiting. As she kissed me, I could think of nothing except how much I wanted to feel her body, how much I wanted to touch her swollen breasts, her heavy, ripe breasts that always strained for my touch, I wanted to slide into her and feel the silk of her pussy.

"Alice," I groaned. "Alice..."

There was something in the way I said her name that ignited the fire in Alice and her kisses became more forceful as she pushed her body into me. We moved backwards, arms wrapped around each other until we reached the car. She opened the back door and we fell onto the seat. The radio was pumping out a mix of late-night dance music, but I didn't want to let go of her to turn it off.

Alice was lying above me and I tore at her coat, desperate to touch the warm skin that was beneath her clothes. Sighs escaped her lips, falling onto mine and I savoured them on my tongue. The intense thirst I had for her was making me ravenous for more. Fuck, I wanted her, wanted to feel her, wanted to fuck her, wanted to kinky the shit out of her, wanted to make love to her. Alice shrugged her wet coat off and dumped it on the floor as I reached for her tee-shirt, pulling it above her head.

She was naked from the waist up and my cock hardened further as I looked at her high, swollen breasts and the rosy erect nipples.

"Alice. Fuck, Alice." I groaned against her skin. "Fuck."

Alice leant over me and hungrily I pulled her nipple into my mouth. She tasted sweet and feminine and I held her to me, sucking hard until she cried out. Alice raised her hips from mine and fumbled with her trousers. Letting go of her back, I yanked them down and cupped her arse with my hands. Alice rocked against me, as though asking for more. I gave her a short, sharp smack which echoed in the car, out of time with the music still pumping from the radio.

"Again." She whispered, kissing me. "Again."

I did as she asked, harder this time, feeling the sting in my palm. Alice cried out and I spanked her again, limited by the space in the car, but hard enough for her to gasp, "yes, Lucien, yes."

I freed my cock from my trousers. It was so hard that the ache was a throbbing heat. I had to be in her. I had to feel her pussy clenching around my cock, I had to feel her cum on me, I was desperate.

I held my manhood as Alice moved herself over me and slid down my length so slowly it was agony. The space in the car didn't allow for much movement but Alice steadied herself with the seat in front and began to move above me. It was exquisite to be in her, to feel the strong muscles of her channel holding me as she writhed above me. It was exactly where I wanted to be.

Alice rocked faster against me, her cries getting louder and louder until I felt the quivering in her pussy. Her muscles clenched around me and the intense feeling in my cock increased until the heat exploded from me and I came powerfully into her. Alice moved once more and cried out as her orgasm shook her body. She collapsed down on me. Spent, I wrapped a heavy arm around her.

It was one of the best fucks of my life.

ALICE

At any moment the spell would break, and Cinderella would realise she was naked on the side of an East London street, wrapped in the arms of the man who shattered her heart into irreparable pieces. The same Cinderella would also realise that she had initiated something she would never be able to blame on Evil Prince Charming and she would have to live with her complete fuck up.

The devil had called my name and I handed over my soul.

Again.

What had I been thinking? I moved and Lucien's arm tightened around me.

"Lucien..."

"Shh." He said in reply.

"I want to go." I didn't at all, but I had to find some way of regaining the control I'd dropped outside in the rain.

"You don't. You want to come home with me."

"How misguided you are." I snapped, wriggling under his arms to break free. "That's never going to happen."

"According to you this would never happen and look where we ended up."

"I had a complete leave of my senses. I'd had too much champagne and wasn't thinking clearly." I didn't want to move, my orgasm had left a glow on my skin and warmth in my veins that, complete fuck up or not, was going to be difficult to let go of. Letting go of Lucien was going to be even harder but this was something that could never be repeated.

"You keep telling yourself that Alice." He said with a shrug. "You keep telling yourself that you didn't want it, or you don't want me until you believe it."

I jolted my body and his arms unclasped from behind my back. "I don't want you."

"You are such a liar. Why are you so desperate to convince yourself that you feel nothing for me?"

"Because you broke me." I said with such force in my words that Lucien appeared to shrink under the tone of my voice. I picked up my soaking coat from the floor and put my arms into the sleeves, tensing as the cold, wet fabric touched my bare skin. "You broke everything. It took me months to get over you, you did the cruellest thing to me imaginable and I paid the price for all the lies I told. Karma kicked my arse." I picked up my clothes and bundled them into my arms. "I should never have done this tonight, this is all on me and I will have to live with it. Shit, there is someone who seems to want to be in my life, he likes me, and this is how I treat him? I'm no better than you!"

I scrambled with the door handle and began to climb out of the car, back into the rain. Lucien sat up and tucked himself away. There was a part of me who wanted to go with him, back to his apartment, because a fuck in a car wasn't how the ending should be for us, but I'd lost the control I had when I asked him to spank me and I wasn't giving him any more power over me. The spanking was a punishment for the feelings I still couldn't process, the feelings I had about my fledgling relationship with Zac and the overwhelming feelings I had towards Lucien.

I was a fucked-up mess.

And, it was all my fault.

"Are you, Alice? Are you better than me? Really?"

"I was. Now, I think I'm worse."

"This man you like? Does he know what makes you tick? Does he know the dark side to you, Alice, or are you afraid to show him?"

"It's none of your business, Lucien." I snapped and then the rage left, leaving behind a sadness that twisted my stomach. "Every time I feel at my most vulnerable, you show up. It's like you know." I closed my eyes against the sting of unshed tears. "I can remember asking you if you were the devil, you said no. Perhaps it's me. Perhaps I am." I took a deep breath in. "I don't want to see you again, it's no good for me. You are no good for me."

"Alice?" Lucien said softly. "I only came here tonight because I needed to talk to you, I didn't want to upset you…"

"Then you should never have come."

I slammed the door and ran down the street, holding my clothes tight to me like a security blanket. My feet made a slapping sound on the pavement as I ran, keeping my eyes firmly ahead, never once looking behind me. I wouldn't have any resolve if I saw Lucien watching me.

I cried the whole way home.

LUCIEN

It was a long drive home. I felt like shit. It was as though there was a knife twisting in my stomach, twisting and slicing until I wanted to vomit with the pain of it. I pulled over to the side of the road and opened the window, letting the cold, wet air into the car. Fuck, fuck, fuck. Seeing Alice had not gone the way I'd wanted it to. Of course, sex with her would always be at the top of my list of great ways to end the day, but it had not been what I'd gone to her for. Despite the encounter being hot and fierce and full of emotion, it had left me feeling more bereft that I'd have thought. She was right. I was no good for her.

Yet again, I'd made her cry.

I was a total bastard.

Maybe I should just keep away, leave her to the life she was fighting to carve out of herself. Maybe I was just too old, too bad, too damaged to be in her life. I didn't ever make her happy, just tore away pieces of her time and time again. I rubbed my scar with my forefinger. It was pulling again, the more hurt I caused Alice, the more the scar tightened against my skin. I vehemently hated the vivid and permanent reminder of the hellish mistakes of the past, mistakes from which there could be no escape and ones that would haunt me forever.

I pushed the button that wound up the window. Inside the car the tapping of rain, loud on the car windscreen, sounded as though my demons were knocking to come in. To drown them out, I turned the radio up, but the overnight DJ was too happy, and too enthusiastic about life, to be the right sort of company. Putting the car into drive, I continued across London, my tears falling as fast as the rain outside. I wasn't a man who cried. Not ordinarily, but fuck, my life was like a noose around my neck and I was so tired of it. I was tired of everything. Tired of being me and of the fucked-up person

I'd evolved into over the last decade. I needed a break from everything but until the demons set me free, I feared the rest would not come.

ALICE

"Hi." I said shyly. Zac was sitting at a window table in the café when I walked in. He looked tired and had a bruise on his cheek, but his eyes sparkled when he looked up and saw me. It was nice to have someone sparkle at me. Even if I didn't deserve it.

I'd been to hell and back inside my own head since my dalliance with Lucien on the previous Sunday. I felt like I was two different people, angel Alice and bitch Alice and it was hard to know which one of them was the real me. Lucien had been haunting my dreams so excessively during the few days that had passed, that I barely slept, fearful if what I would see when I closed my eyes.

When I did close my eyes, I saw it all. The first time. The second time. The Cotswold hotel. Paris. Delphine. The Club. The lies. The apartment. My flat – The night endlessly taunted me, showing me all my failings over, and over, again until I wanted to scream. Even trying to switch off with an intimate midnight stroke and some porn just made me think of Lucien and it became his touch, his fingers, his hands. I thought I would have conquered my addiction to him, but it was now worse than ever.

"Hi Alice." Zac said standing up to greet with a kiss on the cheek. His mouth was warm and soft against my skin but the tingle I was hoping for, was absent. It made me think of Olivier and how much I wanted to fancy him. I was surer than ever that I was destined to be alone. "How are you?"

"I'm good thank you." I lied, sitting down. "How are you? How were the few days to the sunshine?"

"Pretty shit." Zac admitted. "I wish it had been a jolly to the sunshine! It wasn't one of the most exciting operations, in and out and that was it. Job done and home. On standby for the next one."

"It must be strange living life without actually knowing what is coming next?"

"Yeah, there are pluses to it, excitement and serving the country and so on, but sometimes it feels as though I've just got back into civvy street and for a moment everything is normal, just like it is for everyone else. Then I'm off again, back to all the stuff that makes my job the best job in the world, but also the hardest. It makes planning difficult and it makes having a life outside of work a struggle too." Zac stared at me with intent in his eyes and I felt my cheeks redden. He smiled softly and I realised that he wanted me to be the 'life' he'd mentioned. Shit, that made me feel worse than ever.

"Did you shoot any baddies?" I asked lightly, changing the subject to take the heat from the air around me.

"I saved the universe all by myself, you can rest easy now!" Zac grinned.

I laughed. "Is that right. Then you must be like a super hero or something?"

"You will never know how super I can be!" Zac scratched the bruise on his cheek. "Or, you may. If you're lucky."

I felt hot.

Zac grinned and said, "Saffron told me that you'd been nominated for an award. You must be really pleased."

"Yeah," I said, trying to add some enthusiasm to my voice. "I am. It's a huge deal even to be nominated. Saffron thinks she's going to get some staff to boss around because she's sure I'm going to win. I don't think I've got a hope in hell though, but we'll see."

"I'm sure you have. Saffron has faith in you, perhaps you need some faith in you." His blue eyes twinkled as he handed me a menu.

"Yeah, maybe!" I took the menu and glanced at it. "The prize money would be good! Saffron has already spent her share I think!"

"What would you do with the prize money, if you won"? He asked.

I let out a big breath and said, "I'd go on holiday. Anywhere hot, tropical and quiet. Somewhere that no one could find me for a couple of weeks, I'd switch off my phone and just sleep. It's been a long time since I slept well." I grinned. "It's not very imaginative but it sounds so blissful, I almost hope I win!"

"Do you not want to win, then?"

I thought for a moment and then replied, "it would be a huge honour, the directors of some of the biggest businesses in London vote and that kind of recognition can change a small business overnight." I shrugged my shoulders. "I'm not sure I'm ready to go from small to potentially huge as quickly as winning the award could make it happen. I'm so happy with how things are, and I love working at the Hub and having Saffron help me, that to suddenly have more, I'm not sure it's for me."

Zac looked at me curiously.

"Do you think it's strange?" I asked him. "Strange not to want to grow fast? Saffron does…"

"It's your business." Zac said. "I think it has to run however you want it too. It's hard to know, really, in my line of work, decisions like that are made by someone else. We do what we are told to and then we come home. I don't know what life is like on civvy street."

"Tiring." I grinned. "I exist on coffee!"

"It's no wonder that you don't sleep." Zac commented pouring me a glass of water from the jug on the table. "You need green juice and lots of this."

"I'm working on it!"

We had a nice lunch. Zac was funny and interesting and seemed to find my anecdotes about life at The Hub amusing. He was really attentive, but in a way that felt completely alien to me. I'd never had a man that whose focus was solely on me and I didn't know if my responses were the right ones. It felt false somehow and made the guilt sitting in my stomach, so much worse. I flirted and flicked my hair and leaned into him when we talked, knowing I was overcompensating because I felt so disgusting for having fucked Lucien in the street. I was too tired to know if Zac noticed anything in my behaviour, but to me there was very definitely a difference.

The waitress put the bill down onto the table and began clearing the plates. "This has been lovely," I said, tying my hair up with a band.

"As always." He said, smiling and stretching out his arms. I stared at the muscles under his tee-shirt that flexed and retracted as he moved. There was definitely a hot, strong body under his clothes, and I felt a faint stirring in my centre. That, I decided, was a good sign, and I leaned in closer and brushed the mark on his cheek. "You're bruised."

He touched his cheek. "Ah, that's nothing! One of those things that happens in my line of work!"

"A hazard of the job?" I asked.

"One of the many." He said, giving me a tight smile.

"Was it harder than you're letting on, then?"

"I wish I could tell you, sorry, Alice, sworn to secrecy!" He yawned. "I, too, am tired, my body clock doesn't know where I am!" His phoned beeped and he picked it up from the pile of his items in the window sill. Zac looked at the message and frowned. "Bugger, work calls, I'm going to have to go."

"Are you going somewhere?"

"I don't know yet. Need to make a call, my life isn't my own! Rather like owning your own business, I'd imagine! Shall I walk you back?"

"No, it's ok thank you. I have a few things to buy, I'll go back via the shops." I left some notes with the bill and stood up. "I feel the need to delay the return to work, my to-do list would scare even Dracula!"

Zac laughed and leaned into me. Lightly he brushed a stray hair from my face and kissed me.

I felt something. It was tiny, but it was there.

***

"You'd better buy a dress and brush your hair!" Saffron squeaked as I struggled into our cubicle under a number of supermarket bags. I'd lost the feeling in two of my fingers and I rubbed them frantically to liven then up.

"Why?" I was distracted, wondering if my guilt had led to Zac thinking I was acting strangely.

"Because we're off to The Hampton Hotel!" Saffron's excitement sent her voice several octaves higher. "You've been nominated. Can you believe it? You're up against two other young entrepreneurs, isn't that amazing?"

"Have I? Really?" I had a flicker of the excitement that Saffron was exuding until I remembered that Lucien was one of the key decision makers and I suddenly felt flat. "I have a dress."

"Well don't you look a picture of happiness." Saffron remonstrated. "There I was getting all excited and feeling proud of you and you look like the world's most miserable person." She looked so disappointed that my heart sank.

"Sorry Saff." I said sheepishly.

"I should think so! How was lunch with my dear brother? Is it true love yet?"

"I don't think so…"

"Bloody hell Alice, what is the matter? You've just had lunch with my handsome, heroic brother, you've been nominated for an amazing award, which you'll win and you're looking as though you've lost your last pound down a drain. Seriously, you need to cheer up or I'm going home! I can't work in an environment like this, your aura is so negative that you're squashing every creative bone I have!"

"You do admin…"

"Creatively!"

I laughed. "Yes, you certainly do the admin creatively! You can go home Saffron. I'm going to go home too, there are things I can do there, I don't need to be here. Take the rest of the day off, go be wild with your crazy friends. You may never be able to have a day off again, if we win!"

"Really?"

I nodded.

"Thanks Alice." Saffron said, turning to her computer and saving all her documents. "You could always call Zac!"

"I think he may be busy."

"Oh?"

I shrugged and yawned loudly. "He headed off very quickly after lunch."

Saffron looked confused. "Did he? He told me he was free all day, I wasn't expecting to see you back."

"He got a message, a work call, he said."

Saffron shrugged. "Life with Zac, something always comes up. Who'd be in the forces, hey?"

"Not me." I said, swivelling on my chair to face my laptop. "Go home, Saff."

"See you tomorrow, Alice."

"See you tomorrow."

LUCIEN

The hotel ballroom was buzzing with voices as I made my way down the grand staircase. I scanned the room over and over looking for Alice, but the sea of people was too thick for me to see anyone's face properly. I usually hated award evenings. Lots of back slapping and fake shows of friendship between rivals before they all got outrageously pissed and the gloves came off.

I avoided them ordinarily but tonight was different. I'd not seen Alice, or sought her out, since the fateful Sunday evening. I wanted to, the longing to tell her everything woke me up from the endless nightmares and I wondered if, by telling her the absolute truth, it would make any difference and I could finally sleep.

Leave me alone. She'd said over and over, yet every time her actions betrayed her words. If it had been anyone else, perhaps I'd have listened but there was something about Alice that I could not let go of.

Nor, it seemed, could she let go of me.

Of all the women I'd known and fucked in the past decade, and there had been lots, Alice was the one who made my cock so hard that it caused a discomfort bordering on pain. A pain that only Alice could relieve, I know because I tried. I got hard every time I thought of her soft, naked body. I got hard when I pictured her high, ripe breasts. I got hard from the memory of the delicious moans that she uttered when I hit her sweet spot. Everything about Alice made me hard and even the endless wanking could not take away the ache.

I craved her, physically and mentally. She was the only one to stand up to me, to demand that I give more than I had ever intended. I know why I left her in Paris, but I still questioned myself for it and I still hated myself for causing her to hurt like I did. I wished, more than anything, that I could take away the memory of seeing her with Delphine, tied up and blindfolded, looking as sexy as fuck. She should have been with me, that show should have been for me, for her, for us.

I was stopped a number of times on my way to my seat by business men and women I'd had dealings with over the years. I maintained a conversation for as short a time as I could get away with and moved onwards through the crowd.

It was going to be a long night.

"Good evening Mr Ross." Declan Manvers, the hotel General Manager greeted me with his hand outstretched.

"Good evening Declan." I said taking his hand. "I am surprised to see you down here this evening."

"I like to oversee these events," he said smiling. "It does wonders for bookings!"

"I can imagine." I looked around at the tables. "I don't suppose you could do something for me?"

"Of course."

"Can you move Alice Addison and her guests to my table."

"Alice Addison?" Declan looked confused. "That's not a name I am familiar with."

"She's one of the nominees."

"Mr Ross, we don't usually…"

"I'm pretty sure you could this time? No nepotism, I can assure you that I didn't vote for her."

Declan looked unsure but said, "I'll see to it, Mr Ross."

"Thank you."

I walked past my seat to the bar at the back of the ballroom and ordered a whiskey. It was the first drink I'd had since Alice dragged me from the dive bar, but suddenly I needed the courage that came in the form of the amber liquid. I should have left well alone, she would almost certainly have whoever he was with her and I wasn't sure I could hold back if he were too close.

I have someone in my life, she'd said. I ordered another drink.

***

"Ladies and gentlemen," the Master of Ceremonies called, rapping a wooden hammer onto a board. "Please be seated, dinner is served."

I put my glass down on the bar and chucked a bank note beside it before crossing the ballroom. I could see my table filling up and slowed my pace until the last seat, bar mine, was taken. Alice looked around nervously, the name card in her hand and confusion in her eyes. A waiter gained her attention with wine bottles and she accepted the white wine before taking a long drink from her glass.

"Good evening everyone." I said smiling to the table as I took my seat. "I trust you are all well?"

I heard Alice mutter under her breath and look towards the man she was with. The yellow-haired girl on the other side of him smiled at me and I introduced myself.

"Oh, Alice used to work for you." She said in reply. "Nice to meet you, I'm Saffron, Alice's assistant and this is my brother, Zac." The brother extended his hand and proffered pleasantries, that I returned, far friendlier than I'd imagined my response to be. Alice took a deep breath in and turned to me.

"Good evening Lucien. How surprising that I ended up sitting by you."

"Imagine my good fortune, Alice."

"Imagine." She said stiffly, picking up her glass and downing the remaining liquid. Zac looked questioningly at her and she smiled at him. "Wine?" She asked.

"Yes please." Zac said, handing Alice his glass. She grinned as she took it and filled it up, but the smile didn't reach her eyes and the nervous biting of her lip and shaking of her hand, gave her away. Perhaps only to me, but it was enough.

Zac moved his head towards her and said something that she laughed at. I felt the hot hand of jealousy grip my heart so tightly it was a physical pain. Bastard.

I watched them carefully. Alice was making a great show of leaning into him and giving him her full attention. She was trying so hard that she didn't seem to notice that his thoughts were elsewhere.

"So, Zac, what is it that you do? Are you in business?" I asked lightly as Alice tensed beside me.

"I'm in the forces and unfortunately for the conversation, that's as much as I can tell you."

"I've done a lot of work for the military," I told him. "I completely understand the need for secrecy. It doesn't make well for relationships though, does it? All the secrets. Can you imagine keeping secrets Alice?"

"Alice is an open book!" Saffron interjected enthusiastically. "Everyone knows everything about her!"

"Is that so? No secrets, Alice? You must be the only person I know who doesn't have any." I said, leaning forward and running my fingertip up her thigh. Her leg was covered by the table cloth and kept my deliberate action hidden, but the subsequent yelp and sloshing of wine had her leaping from her seat.

"Alice? Are you ok?" Zac asked mopping up the spilled wine with his napkin.

"Yeah, yeah I'm fine." She said, flustered, holding her hand to her chest. "It felt as though there was something really creepy on my leg, but it must have been my imagination."

"You're so random!" Zac said affectionately, refilling her glass.

Alice sat back down and ground her sharp heel into my foot. "Do that again," she hissed angrily, "and I will accidently stab a fork into your groin."

"I don't think that's really what you want to do to my groin." I said out of the corner of my mouth. "I think you'd much prefer to have your face in it."

"You make me sick." Alice snapped and turned to Zac.

I grinned.

"So Zac, tell me, how did you and Alice meet?"

Zac looked from Alice to me and replied, "through my sister."

"I'm not sure that it's any of your business, Lucien." Alice snapped, interrupting. "Although, I'm surprised you didn't know, given your interest in spying on people."

Zac gave me a long, hard look. "I don't spy." I told him. "We do lots of work for the military and we have to run background checks before employing people. Alice objected and seems to have me pegged as a spy." I laughed. "Perhaps she just has something to hide."

"Do you always make people feel uncomfortable, Mr Ross?" He asked in a tone that gave no illusions as anything other than a threat.

"Not ordinarily Mr…"

"Eaton." Zac replied. "It seems you are doing just that this evening."

"Not my intention, I assure you." I replied smiling. "I was actually going to complement Alice on her nomination and on how lovely she looks this evening, but I'll leave that to you." I turned my back and greet the man on my right and his wife. I gave the resulting conversation half my attention, whilst texting a brief message to John Frank.

Find out what you can about Zac Eaton, military. I suspect special forces.

On it. John's reply came almost immediately.

I slipped my phone back in my pocket as the waiter brought out the first course.

ALICE

If there was a hell on earth, the ballroom of The Hampton Hotel was it. There were so many people in here that it was hot enough to be the underworld but sitting so close to Lucien was spiking my temperature uncomfortably. I couldn't believe it when the table plan showed my seat next to his, and I realised, with a rapidly sinking stomach, that he had had some involvement in the placing. All the other nominees were sat in a cluster near the front of the ballroom, closest to the stage, where it would be far less complicated to walk up to the podium to receive their award.

I wished that Saffron had never completed the application.

Mostly, I wished that I'd never, ever gone to work for Lucien fucking Ross.

I leaned into Zac, and he took hold of my hand, raising it to his lips and kissing it softly. With Lucien on the other side of me, the spark I wanted with Zac was absent. Fuck, fuck, fuck! I'd wanted to have a lovely evening with Zac, perhaps a late-night drink, perhaps even a night that didn't end until dawn. As much as I tried to focus on Zac, Lucien being so close was a distraction straight from the shores of Hades.

I wanted to die there and then when Lucien ran his hand casually up my thigh. He was being deliberate and calculating, playing me to prove a point. His touch had the affect he had been looking for, the arousal hit between my legs almost immediately.

Bastard.

I had lost my appetite by the time the waiter brought the first course, and the wine was slowly going to my head. I'd had enough of it, drinking it quicker than water, anything to blot out the excruciating closeness to Lucien and the growing coldness that was beginning to radiate from Zac.

"Is that work?" I asked Zac as he picked up his phone again.

"No." He replied, glancing at the screen and putting the phone down again. "A few of the lads are looking at booking a long weekend away."

"Oh? Nice!"

"The headaches that follow aren't nice though!" Zac looked from me to Lucien. "Is he always like this?" Lucien was talking to the woman sitting on his right, but I sensed he had one ear on our conversation.

"Like what?" I asked, feeling an anxious squirm in my belly.

"Always so…I don't know, doubled edged."

"Double edged?"

"Yeah, everything has two meanings, have you noticed?"

I shrugged as nonchalantly as I could manage. "I try not to pay him much attention."

Zac looked at me, his head cocked to one side and it felt as though he didn't quite believe me. He flicked his eyes across to Lucien and I had the sense that they were having a stand-off. I felt my skin redden and my palms were suddenly damp. From somewhere a little voice whispered, *this won't end well.* With a slight shake of his head and a deep sigh, Zac turned his attention back to his phone.

"I thought you said he was interested in you." Lucien murmured.

"Go to hell." I snapped, standing up abruptly. To Zac and Saffron I said, "please excuse me," as I turned and rushed from the ballroom, across the expansive foyer and into the ladies' room. The temperature was cooler in there and I leaned my burning face against the mirror. I squeezed my eyes shut to stop the tears from falling. My makeup had been expertly applied by the beautician, Ali, whose salon was along the road from my flat, and there was no way I was going to ruin two hours of her work over Lucien sodding Ross.

"Alice?"

"Go the fuck away, Lucien." I said wearily and then I burst out into mirthless laughter. "You know, before I came to work for you, they said you were a bastard. Then, I discovered that you were worse than they said, but, honestly, tonight, you have sunk to depths I could never have imagined anyone sinking and now you have ruined my evening by rearranging the seating. Why would you do that? What have I ever done to deserve this torture?" I whispered. "I must be a really bad person. You know, all I wanted from life were great friends, a great job, the kind of job that I looked forward to going to every single day, and a great man. Nothing more than that. Nothing beyond what I thought was achievable or that I deserved, but, just as soon as I think I am getting somewhere, you turn up to shit all over me. My parents suggested I move back to Bath, perhaps they're right..."

"Alice?"

"Please don't, Lucien. Don't say anything. Don't try and brush off what you are doing. You didn't need to stroke my leg, you did it to prove something to yourself, you did it to get one up on me and one up on Zac. He's decent, he doesn't deserve what I've done to him."

Lucien's phone beeped and he pulled it from his pocket to read the message. I took my chance to leave the ladies' room but as I passed, Lucien grabbed my arm.

"How do you know he's as decent as he seems?"

"What the fuck is it to do with you?"

"It just is."

"He's not you, Lucien. That makes him decent in my book."

I dragged my arm sharply back from Lucien and walked from the ladies' room across the foyer. I was so tempted to jump in one of the taxis that was idling outside the rotating door, instead I walked back into the ballroom and made my way to the table. Zac and Saffron were talking to each other, and from the way they were holding themselves, it wasn't a peaceful conversation. I sat down in my seat just as the waiter brought out the next course.

"Are you ok, Alice?" Saffron asked me, giving Zac a death stare.

"Yes thanks, I just needed some air." Zac filled my glass and I smiled at him. "Thank you." Lucien didn't return to the table for the main course and whilst in part I was relieved, there was also a part of me that barely breathed. I felt as though I was waiting for the next axe to fall and that he may just be the executioner this time. I forced myself to eat my meal but each mouthful was hard to swallow and sat like a brick in my belly.

As dessert was brought out, Lucien came back, a whiskey in one hand and his phone in the other. He sat down and gave Zac a long look before opening his mouth to speak.

I didn't give him a chance to say anything as I placed my hand on top of Zac and gave him a big smile. "Doesn't the dessert look delicious?" I asked musically, piercing the chocolate shell with my spoon. Zac was staring at Lucien and there was a realisation in his face that I was fearful of. I felt my heart sink.

"So, Zac, do you go away often?" Lucien asked, scooping up some of the chocolate pudding onto the small dessert fork.

Zac took a deep breath in and blew it loudly out of his mouth. "From time to time."

"I think Zac has already told you he can't say anything, Lucien. Or did you not pay attention?" I said, with a mouthful of chocolate and turning closer towards Zac, I asked, "are you enjoying the dessert?" Then I noticed that Zac hadn't touched his and had left the spoon lying across the dish.

"And Alice doesn't mind you being away?" Lucien asked again, cracking the chocolate shell. I gnawed my lipstick away from my teeth and tensed.

"My relationship with Alice is of no concern of yours, Mr Ross."

"I was merely making polite conversation, Mr Eaton."

"It doesn't appear that you are, Mr Ross. In fact, it seems that you are asking seemingly innocent questions with barb on your tongue."

I stared at Zac who was glaring at Lucien. I didn't need to turn around to know what look was on Lucien's face. Shit, shit, shit!"

"Yet I wonder," Zac continued. "Just why you would be so interested in Alice and me."

"No interest at all." Lucien said blithely. "As I said, just being polite."

"Zac," I whispered, "just ignore him, this will all be over soon, and we can go."

"Ok." He said and with some effort it seemed, he dragged his eyes from Lucien to smile at me. Saffron didn't seem to notice anything, she was busy talking to the gentleman on her left who was regaling her with something clearly fascinating. The air between Lucien and Zac had dropped to minus degrees and I shivered. Zac pushed his untouched dessert into the middle of the table and refilled his glass of wine. Lucien calmly sipped his whiskey looking like he'd just won jackpot.

I was about to suggest to Zac that we leave when Lord Jeffrey Coleman, Chairman of the Directors of London Commerce walked up onto the stage and tapped the microphone for attention.

"Ladies and gentlemen." He said. "Thank you for joining us this evening on this tenth year of the awards. The standard, as ever, has been exceptionally high and it has given those of us on the board, many a sleepless night."

I zoned out as the long process of awards, nominees and winners began, conscious of Zac looking as though he'd rather be elsewhere and Lucien, sitting looking thoroughly pleased with himself.

"Why are you being a dick?" I hissed from the corner of my mouth.

"I'm not being a dick, Alice, I'm merely making conversation with a fellow diner."

"You must think I was born yesterday! Why are you making trouble?"

"Because you don't want him!" Lucien said, leaning back on his chair and folding his arms. "Your award is next."

"Fuck the award." I seethed, "and fuck you."

"Alice, Alice, always so cross…"

"Finally," Lord Coleman said into the microphone, looking somewhat relieved, "we move onto the award for Outstanding Young Entrepreneur. We are blessed with a wealth of young talent in London and as such, it was a long night deciding the winner. However, it was an almost-unanimous decision that the winner of this prestigious award and the prize of twenty-thousand pounds goes to Miss Alice Addison of Addison Graphics."

LUCIEN

Alice looked completely shocked as Saffron launched herself across Zac to congratulate her. I watched Alice's face fall as she glanced over at me and I knew she thought she had won because of me. Zac gave her a kiss on the cheek and whispered words of congratulations, but the sentiment never reached his eyes and, over the top of Alice's head, he gave me a stare that read *don't even think about it.*

I wasn't sure if he realised that something had happened between Alice and me, or that his intended intimidating stare was merely a warning to back off. John had done his research in a matter of minutes, and there was nothing on him, the man was squeaky clean. Bollocks.

I watched as he helped Alice from her seat and walked her to the stage. Her body language was awkward as they walked through the tables. He wasn't as 'in' with her as he thought, and I doubted very much that they'd had sex yet. There was no spark between them, no little touches, no stolen glances, aside from what Alice wanted me to believe and wanted me to see, years of experience was telling me a very different story indeed.

Alice was speaking hesitantly into the microphone, that every so often omitted a harsh shriek. Each time it did Alice looked more flustered as she offered her thanks to a list of people. My name wasn't included and it hurt more that I could have possibly imagined. Zac looked over at me with a gloating smile and I longed to punch him in his chiselled fucking jaw.

Alice sat back down and placed the statue on the table.

"Congratulations." I said raising my glass, "well deserved."

"There is no shine to this Lucien." She said flatly.

"If that is because you think I influenced the voting, you have no need to worry. I didn't vote for you."

"Oh." Alice flushed and her tongue darted out to moisten her lips. "I thought…"

"You won it on your own merit."

Zac leaned over whispered something to Alice and she looked taken aback.

"What do you mean you have to go?" She asked, clearing her throat. "Now? Really?"

"Walk me out?"

Alice's face had fallen, and she sat picking at the polish on her fingernails looking as though she would cry. "Ok."

Zac gave Saffron a kiss on the cheek and stood up. "See you later Sis."

"I can't believe you're going." Saffron replied to him crossly. "With no explanation."

"It isn't you I need to give an explanation to, Saff."

"Whatever! You're such a shit, Zac." She said and turned her back on him.

Alice looked worried and when she caught my eye, I could see upset in the deep blue. She was conflicted and I suspect sitting beside me was the reason for it. She wasn't as cool as she wanted to be, her passion in my car gave away exactly how she felt. I took delight in knowing that Zac didn't have that part of her, that part belonged to me.

She stood up and pushed the worry from her face before deliberately giving Zac a lingering kiss on the mouth and following him across the ball room. I knew it was for my benefit, but it didn't stop the jealousy churning my stomach. When Alice eventually came back, she looked sad.

"Everything alright, Alice?"

"Why wouldn't it be?" She snapped, picking up her wine glass and knocking back the contents.

"Oh, I don't know," I shrugged. "Perhaps because your date has just left."

"Do me a favour, Lucien. Don't ever speak to me again."

"You don't mean that."

She started to speak but seemed to think better of it, instead looked down at the cheque on the table. For a young business it was an impressive amount of money to receive.

"How are you going to spend your winnings, Alice?" I asked brightly, topping up Saffron's wine glass followed by Alice's. I leaned against Alice's soft breast as I poured the wine and smiled when her nipple sprung up against the fabric of her dress.

"Feeling excited?" I murmured. Alice folded her arms across her chest.

"Nothing about you could make me excited." She snapped back under her breath.

"Are you sure about that?" I asked, putting the wine bottle down and, burrowing my hand under the table cloth, I ran my fingertips up her thigh to the soft skin between her legs. She trembled under my touch and closed her eyes as I slowly rubbed her.

The waiter came to clear the coffee cups and brought Alice sharply from her trance.

"I have to go." She stood up quickly and said something to Saffron before walking as fast as her heels would allow to the exit, the award and cheque held firmly in her hand.

By the time I reached the foyer, Alice had gone.

ALICE

What a shitty, shitty night.

I'd walked Zac out after the bombshell announcement that he was going, and we'd stood in the hotel foyer with awkwardness like a wall between us. I knew what he was going to say, his face spoke a thousand words, but when he actually said them, I felt all hope fade.

"I like you a lot, Alice." He'd said looking down at his shoes. "But I get the feeling that there was, or is, something between you and Lucien Ross…"

"No, Zac, no…" I'd tried to interrupt but Zac had stopped me with a look.

"It's ok, Alice. Really. A person would have to be blind not to see it, and it explains a lot." Zac had smiled flatly at me. "I always felt there was something in the way and now I know it was him. I saw how he looked at you, when he didn't think anyone was watching…and his questions…well they gave it all away." Zac moved towards me and dropped a soft kiss on my cheek. "I get the feeling that no one else knows, and that he made it obvious tonight just to get to me. He doesn't look like the sort of man who loses easily." Zac gave a small shrug and I felt such intense sadness and guilt that I couldn't utter a word. "It's better to know now, Alice."

"You've got it wrong." I said weakly. "There is nothing between Lucien and me."

Zac smiled gently. "Perhaps you just don't want there to be, but I think you feel something for him that you will never feel for me. It's a bummer because I like you a lot." He fell silent and I had no idea what to say next. I wanted to tell him he was wrong but the lie, always so ready on the tip of my tongue, wouldn't come. Eventually Zac said, "well done on your win Alice…"

"Is that it, are you really going?" I ignored the congratulations being offered. My heart was pounding against my ribs and I willed myself to set things right, to disprove everything he'd said, but the words remained unsaid.

"Yes." Zac nodded and reached out to squeeze my hand. "No man wants to be second best."

"Shit, I'm...I'm sorry Zac, really...shit, I feel terrible, I didn't mean for any of this to happen..."

"There is no need to be sorry, I'm fine." He'd smiled at me and continued, "and I've really enjoyed spending time with you. It's just not meant to be." He'd kissed my cheek and the regret I felt was like a stone laying hard in the centre of my belly. I watched him walk away, through the revolving door where the doorman hailed him a cab. I'd stood in the foyer until the taxi taking him home was out of sight then returned to the ball room feeling bereft.

I thought I'd finally met someone who was decent and who liked me but instead I blew it because of Lucien fucking Ross. I wanted to blame it all on him, because as always, he managed to have me trembling at his touch, and have my body craving his, and because this time it ruined my chance for happiness. But there was no one to blame but myself. I felt dreadful about Zac, his kindness to me was undeserved particularly as he'd had to suffer the indignities of the evening. I'd wanted Zac to have been the right one, the one I'd been waiting for all these years, instead he'd left me, and it was all my fault.

The evening I'd been dreading had lost its shine and the award, coveted by so many, felt like a noose around my neck. I thought about the cheque. At least Saffron would get her New York trip but as for me, it was destination unknown.

My little flat was in darkness when I arrived home. Xander had moved out, sailing on a sea of our mutual, and very drunken, tears and with Zac gone, my loneliness felt extreme. I turned on the lamps and crossed the messy lounge to my bedroom. I got out of my dress and shoved it in the wash bin before slipping on my pyjamas and scrubbing my face clean of the makeup that Ali had so expertly applied.

Underneath all the paint, I look tired and pale and actually, as I studied myself in the mirror, I looked thin. It wasn't a good look on me, but I quite often forgot to eat because I was so busy. I sighed loudly. I was desperately tired and running on empty. There was very little left to give to anyone or anything. I'd tried to venture back into the world, but I felt like an outsider, distant from real life and trapped inside my exhausting bubble of work-insomnia-work.

What I needed was a complete break, some sunshine and time away from everything that I was getting so wrong. I needed to be somewhere that Lucien couldn't find me so that I could process all the difficult feelings I had about him and get some closure on the whole pathetic situation. Perhaps my parents were right, perhaps I should move back to Bath, set myself up in a little flat and commute to London when required. It was a nice dream, living somewhere so beautiful, but I had no friends in the Georgian city and would probably end up lonelier than I was in London.

I opened the fridge that was unusually full due to Xander stocking up for me before he left. None of it was what one might consider to be comfort food, so I opened a bottle of red wine. I didn't really need it after the numerous glasses at dinner, but I was comfort-drinking and I no longer had anyone there to criticise me. I took the bottle and my glass into the lounge and turned on the TV opting for a predicable disaster movie.

At some point, between getting home and opening the wine, the heavens had opened, and the rain was clattering loudly against the window. I pulled the blanket from the back of the sofa onto my lap and snuggled down under it, wrapping my hands around the glass as though it were a hot drink. I was sick of the rain, sick of London, sick of working so hard and sick of making shit decisions. If I were honest, I was mostly sick of how easily Lucien could turn me from a feisty go-getter to some pathetic fuck piece that he could use when it suited him.

It suited you last Sunday. Argh. Shut the fuck up.

I put my glass to one side and dragged my laptop across the coffee table until it was open in front of me. Suddenly the lure of a tropical island, warm sunshine and lots of sleep took over and I typed my wish list into google. Before the first explosion had happened on the film, I was booked on a two week, all inclusive trip to St Lucia.

And, I was going the very next day.

Shit!

LUCIEN

"What do you mean she's gone to St Lucia?" I raged. The poor girl looked close to tears and her bright yellow hair seemed to droop. I felt dreadful. "I'm sorry, Saffron, I didn't mean to get cross, it's just I need Alice desperately and her being in St Lucia is very unhelpful."

"That's ok." Saffron replied in a small voice. "Is Alice supposed to be doing some work for you? She didn't say..." She tapped on a spreadsheet and the computer omitted a loud sound. "Oh, you're not on my list, were you meant to be? This ridiculously long list is usually why people get stressed when Alice isn't here. Not because she is bad at the work, or slow, or anything like that." She said quickly, "far from it, usually the client is stressed and comes in being all demanding and grumpy, so Alice spends time she doesn't have on calming them down. I don't know how she does it. I'd punch most of them." She looked at me and smiled. "Not you, obviously."

"Obviously!" I grinned back. "For me, it would be far worse!"

"Well, yeah, from what Alice has said..." Alice's assistant clamped her hand over her mouth, and I felt my grin widen. So, Alice talked about me, that was a good sign! I took it upon myself to sit down in the spare chair, Alice's chair I assumed. "It was very short notice, her going." Saffron said, "I've been fending calls all morning, I'd just assumed you'd be another person wanting something. They all want blood this morning! So, if you're not here for a meeting with Alice, why are you here? I didn't think you and Alice got on...oops, there I go again with my foot in my mouth!"

"It's ok Saffron, you're not saying anything Alice wouldn't say to my face! I needed to speak to her about something."

"Do you want to leave a message? According to her note, she will be back in two weeks, but I can add you to the list of messages and if she rings…not that I'm expecting her too."

"No, it's alright thank you, I can wait. Do you happen to know where she is staying?"

The girl looked at me with questions in her eyes. "I'm not sure what you need Alice for exactly, but I can't tell you where she is. She'd kill me. She needs a break, I think she's had a pretty shitty time of things recently and my brother is being an arse, so I think she has run away for some space. I've never known anyone work the hours she has and not completely collapse in a heap."

"Why has she gone now?"

"She won the award on Friday, which, as you know, came with a lot of money and I guess she decided to spend some of it. She never spends anything on herself so it's a good thing!" Saffron picked up a cheque from the desk and looked faintly embarrassed. "She gave me half, she's such a fool…I won't cash it though, I can't take it from her."

"Why did she do that?"

Saffron narrowed her eyes. "Because she is one of the kindest, greatest most fabulous people I know and because she knew I wanted to go to New York and when I told her I'd entered her, she said I could have half of the prize money for my trip, if she won. I can't take it, though, she worked so hard for this."

"Have you thought that she would be upset if you didn't take it?"

"No, I hadn't."

"She would be."

The phone rang. "Ah fuck that'll be someone else wanting blood, I wish they would all just go away…" Saffron's cheeks flushed. "Oh, God, forget I said that, Alice would go nuts if she thought I was putting off a prospective client."

"Don't worry, I won't tell on you!"

"Thanks." Saffron picked up the phone and answered it in a sing-song voice, very different to the stressed one she used when I walked in.

I tried to see what was scrawled on the pad in Alice's loopy writing and when Saffron finished the call I asked for a business card that were on the desk on the other side of the phone.

Saffron leaned over to retrieve a card from the stand. In the split second that her back was to me, I grabbed the paper from the pad and shoved it into my pocket. I had a starting point. Saffron handed me the card and I thanked her before turning on my heel and leaving The Hub, all the while dialling the office.

"Carol?" I said. "Get me on the first flight to St Lucia."

ALICE

God, it was hot! It was a sticky, breath-taking heat and even the cool air conditioning in the car couldn't take the humidity from the air. I had literally just spent an obscene amount of money to escape my demons, Lucien mainly, and run away to a tropical island that was basking under a blazing sun. Having left the rain and cold of a miserable London, my attire of jeans and a long-sleeved jumper had me soaked in sweat within seconds. I wanted to hang my head out of the window and pant like a dog but didn't dare wind the window down for fear of letting the unforgiving heat in.

I could hardly believe that I'd flown half way around the world on a whim, a whim aided by desperation, wine and a cheque for twenty thousand pounds. The money could have done so much for my business, but it gave me a get-out-of-jail-free card and I took the opportunity with both hands. Mum thought I was crazy and tried to talk me out of it. Clearly, she was facing a losing battle as I sat having a cocktail at Gatwick Airport, but she got more and more irate as I told her, very calmly, that I was waiting for the gate to be shown.

"You are mad, Alice, completely mad. You don't know anyone, it's thousands of miles away and you hear such dreadful stories..."

"Mum, I'll be fine..."

"But," she had said barely pausing for breath. "Dad and I were planning on coming to London to take you to lunch for winning the award. We're so proud of you, we bought our tickets."

"I'm sorry Mum." I didn't feel particularly sorry as I took a drink of my cocktail and popped another peanut into my mouth. "Why not have a trip to London anyway, see a show or something. I need this holiday, Mum, I've had a really tough time and..."

"You need a nice boyfriend..."

"Seriously Mum," I had spluttered as the peanut caught the back of my throat, "a boyfriend is the last thing I need."

The screen in front of me had finally flashed with the gate number and I finished my phone call with Mum and walked briskly to the gate before I could change my mind. Now here I was, in St Lucia, sweaty, tired, and a little high on the airline's vinegary economy class wine and my only link to the outside world was a phone had gone flat the moment I stepped off the plane, (a phone that I had no intentions of charging).

Anna had thought I was crazy, but then her love life update during my ridiculously early morning cab ride to Gatwick, took the pressure off my craziness. She was happy. How had I missed so much of her life? What kind of friend was I? Anna had understood, accepted my poor excuses about workloads, sympathised a little, then continued with the detailed descriptions of her new man's sexual prowess. By the time we'd ended our conversation with the 'let's see each other more, I love you, you're my best friend, let's go out once a week' type promises, I had sunk into more of a black hole that I'd been in before.

I'd wanted her to help me fall properly for Zac, so I could go home and make it better or start again with him, but as she'd fallen properly for Tom or Toby or whatever his name was, she was only full of 'it has to be right, Alice, it has to feel right' wisdom that didn't help in the slightest. I wanted her to tell me how to make Zac be the one, even though she had no idea that he had someone to measure up to.

I had a fortnight to sort my shit. I just hoped it was long enough.

The driver pulled up to the hotel and climbed out, opening the door for me before walking around the back to retrieve my battered suitcase. If he thought it looked out of place for a five-star hotel, he said nothing, just carried it into the reception and handed it to the porter. I tipped him, hoping it was enough, and he left the front office, whistling.

"I must be mad." I said under my breath, signing the registration forms and handing over my credit card, thinking for the thousandth time that day what the money could have done for me.

"Thank you, Miss Addison." The receptionist said, taking my forms. "Phillip, our porter, will show you to your room."

I smiled at her and accepted the cold glass of juice from a waiting staff member as I followed the porter through the reception. I was too tired to take in the wonder of the rainforest views to one side and the sparkling blue sea to the other as we crossed the foyer of the gorgeous hotel. He walked me down the hill and stopped in front of my room, unlocking it with a card. After he opened the door, he stood aside for me to enter first.

I gasped, clasping my cheeks between my palms as I stared around, open mouthed. I could not have chosen a more perfect hideaway. My spacious room was painted white, with terracotta tiles on the floor and the bed, pushed against the far wall, was covered in a brightly coloured bedspread. Across from the bed was a small lounge and a sofa with cushions that matched the bed. There was no glass in the windows, just wide-open spaces which meant I could see a one-hundred-and-eighty-degree view of the rainforest with the two St Lucian mountains and the gleaming aquamarine sea from wherever I was standing or sitting. I was truly in paradise, and I stood for a few moments beside the open window with my eyes closed, feeling the warm, tropical air on my skin. I could almost feel the breeze taking my troubles away. The moment Phillip left me alone, I lay down on the bed and fell into a dreamless sleep.

LUCIEN

Being trapped inside my own head for eight hours was torture. The female blonde cabin crew supervisor was extremely attentive, too attentive really, refilling my whiskey glass each time it was drained and giving me the sort of looks I would have once relished. I had fleeting images of her on her knees, arse in the air, waiting for whatever I decided to do to her, but those thoughts didn't last long, and the grim mood set in.

What the fuck I was doing flying four thousand miles to find Alice when she'd obviously run as far away from me as she'd hoped to get. This was a brand-new level of low, even for me, and if I could have turned the plane around, I would have. The whiskey wasn't alleviating the black mood that had increased the further away from London we got and despite all the first-class luxuries, I spent the entire flight despairing.

I was a complete arsehole.

Alice deserved to be happy, but I knew it wasn't Zac Eaton that could make her happy. Watching their interactions, it was obvious that Alice liked him, but it wasn't enough and while he would probably give her a happy life, he couldn't give her what she craved.

I thought back to Friday night. I should not have touched her because feeling her tremble under my caress made me want more. I got hard just thinking about it and lowered the small airplane table to cover my erection. It was wrong of me to do that to her, to put her in that position, particularly as it was so deliberate and premeditated. I was a cunt. Everything about my actions that evening was despicable and showed even more sides to the Lucien that I no longer wanted her to see. I didn't want to give her the chance to be happy with another man and, if I were completely honest, I wanted to prove to her that it was me she desired and that, even though she was with someone else, I could make her long for me.

She didn't deserve that shit from me. I should have just left her alone. Once upon a time, I was a decent guy, I treated everyone with respect but situations and events can change a person and I sat back and watched as my soul slipped away. I didn't want to be this Lucien, the one that broke people, I wanted to be the Lucien I used to be before my life turned to darkness. I could be that person again if Alice let me in.

Of course, Alice could tell me to fuck off and there was a massive risk that me being in St Lucia would destroy the peace that she left London to find. With that thought, my cock went flaccid. Her parents wanted her to move back to Bath and my arrival could be the push she needed. I took out the address John had given me from my wallet. The writing had faded, not that I needed the address, I knew where Ottie was, and it wouldn't be long before it was no longer legible. If Alice refused to give me a chance, then I had to make that terrifying journey alone and I had no idea what would remain of me afterwards.

I'd hidden from my past for so long. Isabelle had taken what had remained of my life and run as far from me as she could have gotten. I would have John looking for her until the last breath left my body, but the pain of having lost everything never went away.

It was all my fault.

The Captain announced over the microphone that we would be descending into St Lucia and I clipped my seatbelt together and sat back in my seat. The blonde supervisor passed by and gave me a smile that told me exactly what she wanted as she slipped a card onto the small shelf beside my seat. I pondered calling her if things went tits up with Alice, so I put it inside my wallet and leant my head back, closing my eyes.

I'd know soon enough if this had been the biggest mistake of the last decade.

I wondered if it was too late for me to make a pact with God. I had no soul left and I didn't think he'd listen, but I asked anyway.

***

It was ridiculously hot. The air was stifling, and my driver was warning of a tropical storm coming to hit the island. If I'd hoped for a little sunshine, I was going to be severely disappointed, although what I really hoped was for time in bed, or anywhere she chose, with Alice.

I'd booked into the sister hotel of the one she was staying in. It was at the top of a hill and the kind of deluxe hideaway where one didn't need to leave. With a butler service and a twenty-four-hour menu, the hotel was designed for lovers. Not broken, middle aged men with a dark past. I stared tiredly from the window of the private car and it crossed my mind for the umpteenth time, that I'd made a mammoth mistake in following Alice here.

I wondered what she was doing. Was she thinking about Zac, was she thinking about me, was she not thinking at all? If I all could do was tell her what haunted me and ask her to hold my hand for one very difficult moment, if that's all she would give me, then it would have to be enough. I promised the heavens if Alice turned me down, I would leave her alone. For good. She would not see me again.

If she refused to listen or rejected me, and meant it, then I would have no other option than to step out of the rat race and sort my shit out. My past had been a noose around my neck for a decade, but I wasn't sure I was able to let it go. I needed to be forgiven before I could move forward but it was far too late to ask Ottie for her forgiveness. I was holding onto the hope that if Alice could still look me in the eye once I told her everything, then that would be enough, for now at least. *What if she rejects you,* the voice whispered? It was what I feared, despite the arrogance and conceit I'd projected in all areas of my life, being rejected by the one person I needed the most would bury any chance of the real me coming back. I wasn't even sure if I would recognise him after so long.

I smiled as the idea that I would do what Alice had done and run away, popped into my head. Perhaps I'd book somewhere to be alone, a Buddhist temple retreat or some other hippy shit that could help me let go. It couldn't be worse than the whiskey-hell I'd let myself fall into until recently.

Whatever happened and wherever I ran to, I had to see Ottie first, that was for sure. I would leave the team looking for Isabelle until they'd searched every single corner of the planet and started over again - if that's what it took to track her down. It sickened me that Isabelle held the key to my forgiveness. It all rested on her.

Bitch.

***

"A friend of mine is staying in your sister hotel, but her phone isn't working so I've been unable to contact her to tell her I've arrived. Would you please check which room she's in please? Alice Addison. A, d, d, i, s, o, n." I waited for the receptionist on the end of the phone to tap on a computer. I wasn't expecting her to tell me anything more than Alice was in the hotel down the hillside, but it was worth a shot. While I waited, I stared across the infinity pool to the tall, proud mountains. I fully understood why Alice came here, there was something so soothing about the view.

I couldn't take my eye from the world outside of the window – the mountains in front, the rain forest on my left and the endless blue ocean to my right. Even for a hard-nosed, miserable, disillusioned fuck-up like me, the island had something special.

"I'm sorry Mr Ross, I'm afraid I'm not able to give you that information, however I believe that Miss Addison is currently on the beach, if that helps?"

"Thank you, yes it does." I replaced the receiver and pulled on shorts and a tee-shirt. Suddenly, I felt the twist of nerves in the pit of my stomach. *Here goes nothing.*

ALICE

I'd slept for fifteen dreamless hours and woke up with a jolt, unsure where I was. I lay in bed waiting for my racing heart to return to normal before wriggling to sit up and gasping as I took in the views. It was a perfect tropical morning. Fresh warm air came in through the open spaces and brought with it the salty scent of the Caribbean sea. I felt the tension begin to leave my body, and when I got out of bed to make a coffee, I already felt as though I was standing straighter and breathing deeper.

It was absolutely the right thing to take a break from London.

Coffee made, I sat in the chair and looked out across the water to the horizon line. I was free. My phone was in my bag, flat and that was how it was going to stay. I'd brought pads and pencils at Gatwick, acutely aware of what my work load would look like when I got back to London, but apart from opening my laptop to send *I've arrived* emails, it, too, would spend the next two weeks switched off. It was a great feeling.

I watched the waves loll onto the sand. It was so unhurried in its rolling that the remaining tension in my stomach dissipated the longer I sat, and I felt energised in a way I'd not for months and months. It was too perfect a scene to remain in my room, that I left my coffee on the table and after a quick freshen up, I took the path down to the beach.

The sand was crunchy under my toes as I almost skipped to the nearest sun lounger, my pad and pencils under one arm and a book I'd bought at Gatwick, under the other. Immediately I was scated a waiter came over with iced water, which I accepted before lying back on the seat and raising my face to the air.

It was so peaceful. The beach was almost empty and aside from a couple of speedboats that passed by, there was no vehicles to be seen. The outside world no longer existed, the noise and sounds and smells of London were already a distant memory. Apart from the calls between staff and the buzzing of the St Lucian wildlife, there was nothing to disturb my peace until my stomach did an almighty rumble and I realised I was starving. I supposed I should have gone in search of breakfast, it was still early enough, but I was so warm and content on my sun lounger that I didn't want to move for fear of losing the feeling.

But, of course, all good things have to end.

"Hello Alice."

I stared up at Lucien with disbelief. He was looking down at me, uncertainty in his eyes and at least had the good grace to look nervous. I felt a surge of intense rage replace the contentment and red spots began to cover my vision. I wanted to scream and let the anger I was feeling explode from me like a hurricane. The sky seemed to turn dark and from somewhere a loud crack of thunder echoed across the bay as I froze with shock.

"What the fuck." I whispered, screwing up my eyes until I could only see the blackness, hoping he would be gone when I opened them again. He wasn't.

The clouds that had swept in, without me even noticing, dropped great splodges of rain onto the beach. Ignoring Lucien, I picked up my book, pad and pencils and hurried across the beach, the crunchy sand sticking to my feet as I quickened my pace. All I could think was, *it wasn't supposed to rain.*

Lucien followed behind me and I could hear his feet on the coarse sand. When I got to the path I broke into a run, up the hill to my room, my head down against the storm. The weather seemed to fit my mood, evil and dark. Bastard. The utter, immeasurable, selfish bastard. He was the devil, there was no other explanation as to the level of torment he was inflicting on me and I wanted to hate him with every breath in my body.

I did hate him.

Only it wasn't enough.

I reached my room and fumbled in the pockets of my shorts for my key card. By the time I'd found it, Lucien had caught me up.

"Alice." When he said my name, it was the tone of desperation in his voice that made me turn around to face him. "Alice, please…"

I wanted to punch him in the face and pound him until he felt as shit as me. "How dare you come here, how fucking dare you. I came here to find some peace and you can't even let me have that. What next Lucien? What torment are you going to subject me to next? You made a choice, you left me, Lucien, alone, in Paris. Have you forgotten that? And now you don't leave me alone, ever. When will you realise that I want to live my life and find someone who will treat me well, I deserve that to have that, I'm a good person, most of the time. I thought I'd found that person in Zac, but it went wrong, because of you."

I didn't want to cry but the tears spilled, fighting with the rain for room on my cheeks. Lucien looked as desolate as I felt.

"I came here to talk to you, because, I'm going fucking crazy." He raked his hands through his hair until it stuck up at all angles, soaked by the storm. "I'm going crazy without you, Alice. I know I shouldn't have come, it was a risk, but I had to see you. Not to be a weird stalker or any of the other things you call me, but as Lucien, the real me. The Lucien I have never let you see."

"I don't want to see another Lucien." I hissed through gritted teeth, holding back the sob that was swelling in my throat. "I don't want to see this one." I gestured up and down at him. "You ruin everything." I couldn't breathe, the lump in my throat and the wound in my chest was preventing any air from getting into my lungs. The world around me began to spin and I grabbed at the door to save myself from collapsing under buckling knees.

"I know." Lucien's reply was barely audible against the pounding in my ears. He was going to break me completely and the St Lucian dream had ended before it had a chance to begin.

"I can't do this, Lucien. I can't go over old ground with you, over and over, you're sending me insane. You left me." I shook my head, "but the way you're acting, it's as though I did something unforgiveable to you." I took a big, shuddery breath in, followed by another, followed by another until the world righted itself.

"I'm not here to send you insane, Alice, I'm here because I need you."

"You need me? *Need me?* Since when did the almighty Lucien Ross need anyone?"

"Since I met you." Lucien spoke so quietly and the truth in his words rang as loudly as a peel of church bells. I took a step backwards, my retort dying on my lips as I stared at him. The scar on Lucien's face stood out red against the slowly paling skin of his face. "You changed everything." He said, closing his eyes. "I hid behind the image of Lucien Ross for a decade, and it wasn't until Paris that I stopped hiding. That's why I left. No one has seen the real me in a very long time, so long that I had no idea how to even be me." Lucien rubbed his hands over his eyes and took a deep breath. "I didn't come here to fuck up your holiday, Alice, I came here to tell you everything, to ask for your forgiveness, to ask for your help, but not to make you cry. I didn't want to fuck up your life, even though I know my behaviour has been despicable." A small smile curved his lips. "I will admit that I did want to fuck up Zac Eaton's chances with you though."

"You did that alright."

Lucien shrugged. "You don't need someone that perfect. Where's the fun."

I glared at him. "But I need someone imperfect like you? Is that what you're implying?"

"Yes," he said slowly. "I know you want me and even though you're as mad as hell and wishing a lightning bolt would strike me dead, you still want me just like I want you..."

"So what was Paris then? A figment of my imagination?"

"Paris was me trying in my own way to protect you..."

"By leaving me in a hotel room in the middle of the night, for Delphine to float by and antagonise..."

"You went with her, it didn't look as though you were under duress." Lucien snapped, "I saw you. You were naked in a room full of strangers, for fuck's sake Alice, do you know unsafe that was?"

"You were there too." I whispered. "I know you were there."

"I was. I went for the same reason that you did – to get plastered and fuck someone to forget, but like you, I couldn't." Despite the rain I felt the heat over my skin as Lucien moved closer to me. "I couldn't do it Alice, I didn't want to fuck any of them."

I closed my eyes and then with a deep breath, said, "but you did fuck the other women though, didn't you Lucien? The woman in the message, and who knows how many..."

I screwed up my face as Lucien replied, "yes I did." His honesty cut like a serrated knife through my stomach and I wrapped my arms around myself to hold my insides together. There was nothing else to say to him, this man I loved. The truth was salt in my gaping wounds.

"Alice." He said pleadingly. "They were agreements, that's all, hangovers from my past..."

"That's all I was." My voice broke as I spoke, and I wanted to vomit.

Lucien shook his head sending rain droplets into the air. "That's what I said, to keep you away, I didn't want you to get close. I hurt people, Alice. It's why I chose the life I did, agreements, women to fuck, it kept everyone safe from me. I wanted you to be safe."

I opened my eyes and glared at him. "That has to be the biggest lie of all."

LUCIEN

Alice was glaring at me, ice dripping from her eyes. The tears that were falling dried up almost immediately and the feisty Alice was back. I barely had seconds to convince her to hear me out before my time was up. Something closed in her face and the tick tock of the clock seemed to speed up.

"Alice. I came here to tell the truth. To tell you all the shit and give you all the reasons why I tried to let you go and failed miserably."

"I need this holiday so much," she whispered, her face paling worryingly. The rain had stopped as quickly as it had started, but she was soaked to the skin and despite the warm temperature, she was shivering. "It was my chance to figure out the craziness in my head and have a break from everything, from me, from what I've done, from you and the endless games you seem to want to play...I came here to sleep." She looked me straight in the eyes and I could see the tiredness in the blue of hers. She looked exhausted and it was all my fault.

Alice continued quietly. "Do you know that I've not slept in six months Lucien? I work until I can't keep my eyes open just to keep you away. You're always there. I close my eyes and I see you leaving me in Paris, I wake up in the middle of the night from dreams where you've slammed the door in my face...I came here because I was on the verge of collapse and now you've ruined it all."

I reached for her hand. She didn't tear it away like I would have expected so I held her cold palm in mine. I moved closer, not that she seemed to notice, her eyes were fixed somewhere else, the past maybe. I was close enough that I could feel the heat from her body and smell the scent of the floral perfume she wore. It stirred something in me so primal that I omitted a loud groan and she turned to look at me.

"Luc..." I couldn't let her finish my name. I dropped her hand and reached for her face, holding the soft skin between my palms as my mouth found hers. I wanted her so desperately that the ache in my groin was unbearable. My cock strained and twitched against my shorts as I kissed her. She must have felt it jabbing into her stomach, but Alice kept her arms loose by her side and her mouth stayed resolutely shut.

"Kiss me." I begged against her unyielding lips. "Kiss me, Alice, please. Please." She was stone, a statue that was so cold I felt a surge of panic, a panic that I'd not felt in a very long time. I was losing her. There was nothing in the way she was holding her body that would suggest she would give into the feelings I'd banked on. The awards ceremony could have been a lifetime ago, her body trembling under my touch could have been in another universe, there was nothing here but a cold, harsh reality.

"Kiss me." I hadn't begged for anything since the day Isabelle left me and took what was left of my shattered life with her, but begging I was. I pleaded with Alice, holding her as tight to me as I could manage. I was overstepping every boundary, I had invaded her space and I was kissing her when she gave no indication that she wanted to be kissed. *You are assaulting her,* the voice screamed in my head, *this is not right.* I stopped and took a step back. It was only then that I realised I'd been crying.

"Alice." I said quietly. "I'm doing this all wrong." I wiped my face with the hem of my tee-shirt and I noticed her eyes flicker to my stomach. Perhaps all was not lost. "I didn't come to mess you around or stop you recovering. I came because I wanted...needed...to tell you why I behaved as I did. Why you have every reason to hate me, but for more reasons that you may think. I know I've screwed everything up, I did that the day you came to work for me. I should have said no to you being there, I should have asked for someone more experienced, but there you were, and immediately you got into my head."

"That's not my fault." She said, twisting the door handle. "I hold my hands up to being partially responsible for what has happened between us to this point right now. I wasn't strong enough to keep away from you, and you took advantage of that. You're everything we're told is wrong with a man – you are manipulative, controlling and a bully."

"I am." I admitted, shame twisting my heart. "I am all those things. I didn't used to be," I gave her a tight smile. "I used to be everything that was right in a man."

"What changed, Lucien?" She asked, chewing on a nail and looking down at the floor. "What could have happened that was so significant it turned you into a complete arsehole?"

"My life imploded, Alice. It went from perfect to hell in the blink of an eye…"

"Cut the bullshit Lucien and either tell me or go the fuck away." Alice's fight had returned, and she stared at me with blazing eyes. "Perhaps this is all part of your manipulative personality, perhaps there isn't anything other than your complete inability to be a decent person." She laughed harshly. "You are walking, talking fake news, Lucien. You have to go. Now. I cannot spend my whole life looking over my shoulder in case you turn up where I don't want you to be. What will it take to make you go away?"

"How do you feel about me Alice?" I asked, feeling my face pale as I spoked. "Can you be honest about that?"

"What difference does it make?" She asked sharply. "In this big game you've insisted on dragging me into, what difference does it make how I feel? It's not real." Alice twisted her hair around her neck. "You're too scared of real, that's why you do what you do, isn't it? To feel for someone would make you vulnerable and you can't bear that, can you? The mighty Lucien Ross being dependent on someone.

Instead you fuck women with no regard at all. You make me sick."

"Miss Addison?" A waiter broke the strange silence that had descended over us.

"Yes?" She replied moving away from me to where he was standing under a tree, no more than five feet from us. I sighed deeply and closed my eyes. My moment had gone. That was it.

"Is everything alright?" I heard him ask quietly.

Alice glanced over at me and said, "yes, everything is fine, thank you, just an argument, nothing more. Thank you for your concern."

The waiter looked at me, his dark eyes narrowing. "Ok," he said to her. "Also, Miss Addison, I wished to let you know that breakfast service will be finishing soon and I noticed you'd not been in to eat."

Alice gave him a beaming smile. "I had completely forgotten. It's no wonder my stomach is growling. I'll be up in a moment. Thank you." The waiter nodded to her and made his way up the hill towards the main hotel.

"Ok, Lucien. You have one minute. One. Not a second longer. What the fuck is it that you want me to know so desperately that you would shit on my tropical escape to tell me?"

I cleared my throat but the lump that was strangling me came back bigger. "Alice, ten years ago my life was completely different, I was completely different. I had not long started the business, it was maybe two or three years old, but it was growing faster than I ever could have envisaged. I was married to Isabelle and we had a great life. The business did so well that we could afford a small chateau in France..."

"Chateau?"

"Isabelle dreamed of living in a chateau, she didn't have a great upbringing and when she was little she used to long to run away to a castle..." Alice's face set hard at the mention of Isabelle, but I continued before she stopped listening. "As well as the chateau, we bought the apartment in London where I lived during the week and I used to travel back and forth, mostly at the weekends. It seemed to work, we were happy, and I thought I had it all."

"How lovely..." She said haughtily. "How lovely to have such a perfect life..."

"It didn't last, Alice. My marriage was failing, and I didn't know how to make it right. Then one day, I lost it all. Isabelle left taking everything with her and I've no idea where she is now. I've spent the past ten years trying to find her because..."

"She came back." Alice snapped, "I saw her. It was the day after you nearly died."

"She did, I know. She came back because..."

"I don't care." She thundered and the veins in her neck popped. She clasped her hands to her chest and shut her eyes tightly. I watched her take a few breaths in and out before she said slowly, "I don't care why she came back. Lucien, either get to the point or go away. I have no need to know how perfectly perfect your life was, because clearly, I was part of the shit bit and that is a kick in the teeth...If Isabelle has that much of a hold on you that she could send you to near death, perhaps you should be with her. If you've got people looking for her, why be here? Why put me through all this crap..."

"She doesn't have a hold on me, she has my..."

Alice put her hands over her ears and shook her head. She seemed to be grasping for words and I watched her, longing to reach out to her. "I can't do this, Lucien." She said eventually. "I can't do this anymore. I had a chance with Zac, and you blew that for me. I'm not the sort of girl for whom men come along very often. I could have had a nice life with Zac, he liked me, he was interested in me for being me, not for being an easy lay who liked spanky-spanky shit. I could have had something that looked like a normal life, not a confusing non-relationship kinky-shit that I had with you…"

"This is going all wrong." I mumbled sadly. "I didn't expect…"

"What did you think would happen?" She snapped, "did you think you could waltz in here, tell me about your wonderful life and then I would bow down and let you do whatever you liked…"

"I didn't come here for that…"

"Oh no, I forgot, you have plenty of willing women…"

"Alice." There was something in my voice that made her stop mid-rant and look at me. Her face, an angry red, paled as my face gave away my desperation. I wanted her to hear me but instead her anger and pain was taking the conversation in a direction from which we would possible not come back from. "What I'm trying to tell you, is that there is a reason that I behaved like I have, this past decade, with women, with you. There is a reason my perfect life imploded and I became the arsehole you hate so much…"

"I don't hate you Lucien." She whispered, the fight leaving her. Alice looked exhausted and when she bit her lip, I realised she was as fractured as I was. "It would be easier if I did."

"I hate me enough for the both of us." I smiled tightly. Her eyes met mine and there was a softness in the blue.

"Why?"

"Because, I killed my daughter."

ALICE

I could hear nothing but Lucien's words. *I killed my daughter* and I had no idea if I'd finally slipped into hell. He looked so desolate that if I were in hell, it was his. I didn't know what to say and Lucien stood, barely breathing, waiting for me to speak. How could I say anything? How could there ever be any words to make a confession like that go away?

All around us the small resort was coming alive again after the brief storm. Guests were wandering past us as they went up to the main hotel or down to the beach, sending smiles of greeting our way. I watched them through envious eyes. It was not the place where one should feel sad, but I was. I was feeling sad and shocked and stunned and had no idea what words to utter.

"How?" I breathed aghast. "How? When?" They were not the right words and Lucien seemed to crumple. I'd never imagined he would be a man that would cry, he was always too controlled for emotion, but there, under the Caribbean sky, the tears rolled down his face in an unending stream. I didn't know what to do.

I reached for his arm, but he didn't notice my touch. He was lost in the past, lost in his grief and in the confession that I didn't know how to process. I wanted to make it better, to see the Lucien I knew, the strong, commanding, charismatic man who got under my skin and never left, but that man was the reason he was here, and I didn't know anything about the one silently crying in front of me.

"We'd been out to friends for lunch." He said distantly. "I'd had one, maybe two glasses of wine, no more - at least, I didn't remember having any more than that. I was always careful, always…" Lucien rubbed his face. "It had been a lovely day. They had laid out a huge table in their garden that was almost bowing under the amount of food, there were a lot of us, I supposed there had to be a lot of food. It was nearing sunset and the children were tired, so we decided to leave and take the scenic route home. Isabelle asked if I was happy to drive, I was, the glasses of wine had been small, just a taster really, nothing like the others were putting away. I don't remember thinking that I would be over the limit, I was always mindful of that. We drove along some winding roads, beside the sea and, even though it was late in the day, it was still so hot, we had the roof of the car down. The girls loved it, feeling their hair swishing around. I slowed for a bend and a car was coming the other way."

Lucien took a deep breath in and shuddered, his hand going to the scar on his cheek. It seemed to burn red the more he spoke. "I don't remember the accident. I woke up on the road, with a searing pain in my cheek and I was soaking wet. It took me a while to realise that I had been lying in a pool of blood. I thought it was mine, but it wasn't it was Ottie's…"

I moved closer to him and reached out for his arm. Lucien didn't seem to notice but I kept my hand on him anyway.

"Isabelle said it was my fault, that I was drunk." He said quietly, shaking his head slowly from side to side. "I swear I wasn't, I swear I would never have put anyone in danger like that, but I remember very little and the memories I do have are hazy. I know I said no to more wine, I know I did, Alice. I never got drunk around the children. Never. I drank water while all the adults I was with got plastered, even Isabelle had had her glass refilled more times than I could count. I was so sure I was ok. Alice." He said pleading as though he needed me to believe him, to be on his side. "I would never have driven if I'd thought differently…" Lucien closed his eyes and the pain in his face twisted my heart. "She said it was me. Her words afterwards, were so accusatory and so vicious that it was obvious that she blamed it all on me. Isabelle seemed to forget I'd lost a child too and I began to dread her coming into the hospital to visit. Each time she came she got nastier and nastier that in the end I asked her not to come. I feared for Hettie to be in such a toxic environment…"

"Hettie?" I whispered. "Who is Hettie?"

"Henrietta. She is my younger daughter, she's fifteen now. I haven't seen her since she was five." Lucien took hold of my hand and twisted his fingers through mine. "Ottoline and Henrietta were my whole reason for being, I adored them, they were the most beautiful girls, funny and sweet and so clever. I was in a coma when Isabelle held the funeral for Ottie and when I finally got out of hospital Isabelle and Hettie had gone. I didn't even know where Ottie was buried."

Lucien looked at me and the pain in his eyes was tore at my heart. "It was my fault. My beautiful, wonderful daughter…it was all my fault."

"You said you didn't drink very much," I whispered to him moving closer. "How can it be your fault?"

"Isabelle said I was drunk."

"How would she know if she was drunk herself?"

"I've driven drunk before Alice, you know that." Lucien said. I dropped my eyes from his. I remembered that hideous night all too well and the images were stamped all over my minds eye. The shock at his driving across London while unable to stand, followed by the fear that he would die of hypothermia was all too clear and would forever haunt me. "I could have been plastered and just not remember."

"The Doctors or the police would have known? They would have done blood tests…"

"We weren't found until hours later, if there was alcohol in my blood, it had long gone. There was nothing on the Doctor's report."

I had no idea what to say. So much made sense that didn't before but his confession left me more confused than ever. Daughters, a wife, a death – I didn't know Lucien at all. I had fallen in love with a man who was a closed book and who I now knew even less about than what I thought I'd pieced together.

"Why did you come here to tell me this?" I asked dropping my hand from his to rub my eyes.

Lucien took a deep breath in and wiped his face with his tee-shirt. I tried not to stare at the taught, toned stomach, and tanned skin, nor the trail of hair that ran from his belly button to below his shorts. I gave myself a shake, *not the time, Alice, not the time.*

"The man I've tasked with finding Isabelle and Hettie found Ottie's grave. It's at a small chapel near our Chateau. I should have known that would be where Isabelle laid her to rest, it's where we got married, where the children were christened, I should have known but I didn't. Another failing." Lucien smiled, "one more to the add to the list."

"Have you been to her grave then?" I asked.

Lucien shook his head.

I looked down at my hands. I wasn't sure how long I'd been wringing them for. "Why?"

"I'm too scared to go alone." Lucien admitted, looking ashamed. "I'm afraid of what I will find, that it will be abandoned and unkempt, but mostly I'm afraid that I won't feel her there. I need her to be there. I need to say sorry. I need her to hear me and forgive me."

"Lucien…"

He squeezed his eyes shut. "So now you know it all, Alice. Now you have more reasons to hate me, to add to the list of everything I've done to you."

"I don't hate you Lucien." I said reaching for his hand. "It would make life easier if I did, but I don't. I'm trying to understand why you have come here, why you needed to tell me all of this…"

"There are lots of reasons, Alice. I wanted you to know it all, I wanted you to understand why I was so unwilling to give you what you needed and why I left you in Paris. I wanted you to know that the unwillingness came from trying to protect you from the person I am, because I break things that matter. It was important that you knew what I meant by that."

"Am I 'things that matter'?" I held my breath as I waited for him to speak. He seemed to be considering his reply and I felt the hope in my belly begin to dissipate the longer we stood in silence. Despite the bombshell, despite the past and the anguish that he carried, I couldn't believe that he would have been responsible for the death of his daughter. *Careful Alice, don't be blinded.* Lucien Ross was a lot of things, but I did not believe that he was capable of what Isabelle accused him of. He had looked too confused when he'd spoken and so certain that he had been sober that I felt the truth in his words.

"Do you remember our last conversation, the one in Paris?" Lucien asked me. I nodded. I remembered every single word he'd said to me. "Do you remember that I said I couldn't wake up with you?"

"Yes, I remember you said that if you did, you would never let me go."

"It was true." Lucien said softly, brushing my hair from my face and cupping my cheeks between his hands, and holding my eyes with his. "If you'll have me, if you can take me with all the baggage and all the demons and forgive me for everything I've done, then I want to spend a lifetime waking up with you."

LUCIEN

Alice didn't look at me. Her eyes were fixed down the hill at the beach where the waves had calmed since the storm ended. I desperately wanted to know what she was thinking but her face was a fixed mask and there was no emotion on it to read at all. I felt my heart sink. Shit, I was too late. She moved slightly when her stomach made a loud rumbling sound and I was horrified that she would have missed breakfast due to my obsessive need to confess everything.

"Alice, are you hungry?" I asked, filling the silence with cracked words. The skin on my face felt tight from where my tears had dried in the sun. *Don't cry Lucien, you don't have that right.* Words from so long ago came back to me and I felt winded by them. Fuck, it was all such a mess and from the coldness coming from Alice I knew I should not have dragged her into all of this. I'd had my chance with her, and I blew it, I'd walked out the door, throwing the safe word that I'd given her, right in her face. I should have saved my confession for my priest, even though I was damned to eternal hell anyway.

"It's too late for breakfast." She said dully.

"Come up to my room," I gestured up the hill to the sister hotel nestled in the trees. "I have a butler and room service…"

"That's nice." Alice said taking a deep breath in.

"Come with me, have something to eat…"

She nodded distantly and I put my arm around her shoulder and guided her up the hill. She was clearly wrestling with herself because I could see the strange looks passing over her face as the mask slipped. She was afraid, scared and hesitant, yet at the same time there were flickers of hope and warmth and, most importantly, belief.

We walked in silence up the path to the suites at the top of the hill. I walked Alice across the wooden bridge to my suite and opened the door. She gasped as she walked inside. At the end of the suite was the infinity pool that seemed to reach out to the sea far below, ahead of that were the Piton Mountains.

"You're so flash." Alice said sighing and slipped off her dusty flip flops. "Flasher than flash!"

"It is lovely but also, it was the only room available, it's not the sort of room for a man on his own!"

Alice looked at me for a moment and seemed to struggle with something to say. "You literally have a palace here." She said eventually as her stomach rumbled loudly. Mine growled in with sympathy. "Hungry too?" She asked.

"Yeah, I've not eaten since I arrived here and I have to admit, I'm feeling a little light headed." I handed her the menu. "Let's eat." Alice chose some items from the long list and I rang the order through to the butler. Alice sat down on the tiles beside the pool and looked over at the mountains.

"It's so beautiful here." She commented with a wistful sigh. "So different to the smog and dirt of London. I wonder how I shall leave at the end of the two weeks. How long are you here for?"

"I don't know. That's down to you." I replied, kicking off my trainers and joining her by the pool.

"Is it? That's a lot of pressure for a girl!" Alice's tone was light but there was hesitance behind her words. I wondered if she realised how much opening up to her had cost me. I'd not let anyone in since Isabelle left, and I was fearful of Alice's rejection. I reasoned that as she was here, in my suite, meant there was some hope, but how much was down to her.

We were both lost in our own thoughts when the Butler knocked on the door to bring the food trolley. Neither Alice or I said anything as we piled our plates and ate in a strange silence.

"I was hungrier than I thought." She said with a laugh, wiping her mouth. "I can't remember the last time I ate that much." Alice stretched and said, "thanks Lucien. I don't think I would have lasted until lunch."

"You're welcome." I replied with a smile.

She smiled back and then it fell from her face. I watched a troubled looked settled on her features and she began to gnaw at her lip.

"Alice?"

"Yeah." She replied somewhat distantly.

"Are you ok?"

"I don't know." She fiddled with her fork until her hand trembled and it fell the to the floor. I was mortified when she began to cry. "Shit." She said, hastily wiping her eyes. "Shit."

"Oh fuck. Don't cry Alice," I said leaping up and wrapping my arms around her. "Please don't cry."

"I can't help it. I think it's stress or…something"

"I take it I'm that 'something'?"

"Probably," she admitted, wiping her eyes on my tee-shirt. "It's been very up and down recently, hasn't it?"

"Not as up and down as I'd like!" I said smiling, hoping to lighten the mood.

"Seriously Lucien…"

She nuzzled in closer and I felt my heart speed up. "Sorry." I whispered.

"What are you sorry for this time?"

"All of it, Alice. Sorry for everything. I'm sorry I treated you badly, I'm sorry I was an arsehole, I'm sorry I tormented you, I'm sorry I came here, well I'm not but I know it wasn't part of your plans…"

"Anything you're not sorry for?" She said softly.

"Yeah, I'm not sorry I fucked up things with you and Zac."

Alice pulled back and looked at me, her eyes were rimmed in red and she looked desperately tired. "Can I trust you?

Really? After everything that's happened, how do I know you won't leave me again?"

I took her hands in mine. "I won't Alice. I promise, I won't. I won't that mistake again."

"Really?" She sniffed and rubbed her eyes. "Do you really promise because I'm not sure I'd survive again."

"Alice." I said leaning in and kissing her lips. "I really, really, really promise."

Alice closed her eyes and took a deep breath in. "Well, Lucien." She said, kissing me before standing up and walking over towards the bed, shredding her shorts and tee-shirt, still damp from the storm, as she went. "You're sure you want to be the one I wake up with?"

"Yes." I said huskily, my mouth suddenly dry as I looked at her semi-naked body."

"Where's the fun in that? How about being the one I stay awake with?"

My mouth fall open as she lay down on my bed, naked and glorious. I felt all manner of emotions as I slowly walked towards her, my cock standing proud. She had accepted me, demons and all, and by lying in a position that could have made her vulnerable, instead just put her in control. I was putty in her hands. I gazed down at her. Alice's eyes were hooded and the blue of her irises were glowing from under her dark lashes. Her breasts were high on her rib cage, swollen and waiting for my touch, the rosy nipples hard and peaked.

"You're so fucking sexy." I groaned as my cock strained and throbbed against my shorts.

"Show me how sexy you think I am," she murmured, rolling her tongue over her lips. I watched transfixed as the pink lips darkened. Alice lazily licked her index fingers and slowly stroked the taut skin of her areola until her nipples hardened so much that they turned almost white. She smiled sexily as a groan escaped my lips and she moved to open her legs.

Her moist pussy lips glistened seductively in the light. I licked my lips, my mouth suddenly dry, as I watched her stroking her ripe body, holding her heavy breasts in her hands, before continuing down to her clitoris. I was spell bound as she began to stroke her nub, cooing and sighing as her solo act brought her pleasure. My cock was so engorged that I couldn't move, the desire I had for her was too painful and I knew, once I got inside her wet, warm channel, I wouldn't last long.

"You're amazing." I moaned moving slowly towards her, peeling my shorts away from my leaking cock. "So fucking amazing."

Alice moved her hands up her body and held them up to grip the back of the bed. Her breasts raised higher and the longing I had to suck on her perfect nipples sent my heart racing.

"Come show me, Lucien. Come and show me what I need."

I took the final few steps to her and looked down on her body. Alice had her eyes closed, a look of bliss on her face as she waited for me. I'd seen Alice naked many times but at that moment I saw everything in a new light. The need for control had gone, I felt unburdened and ready to be the new Lucien. The Lucien that Alice deserved.

Lightly I kissed her calves, rolling my tongue over the backs of her knees and lightly licking the inside of her thighs. Alice couldn't prevent her legs shaking as I nipped at the soft skin and she gasped my name over and over. She wanted me in the same desperate way that I wanted her. I could smell the scent of her channel and it sent lava through my veins and down to the end of my cock which twitched as though possessed. If I entered her now, it would all be over in one thrust, so I pushed her legs apart and placed my tongue on her hot, glistening sex.

Fuck me, the taste of her desire brought out the animal in me as I licked and nipped at her until the juice was flowing from her pussy.

"I want you in me, Lucien, now, before I cum." She groaned, gasping as my insistent tongue brought her almost to the edge. Almost, but not quite. As much as tasting her and turning her crazed with my tongue was exciting, I had to be in her before I came all over the bed. I could feel the fizzing in my cock, the bubbles moving along the shaft.

"I won't last."

"I don't care. Please." It was all I needed. I slammed my cock into her wet channel and gripped her hands with mine. My mouth didn't leave hers as I moved in and out of her. Alice was writhing under me, her fingers clenched around mine as the sounds of her orgasm began to build. It was music to my ears. My name was always on her lips, but it was the cries and gasps and sobs as she came around my cock that sent fire around my body. It took every effort not to cum as the muscles of her pussy held me in place until she had drenched me with her orgasm. It was only when her frantic breathing quietened down and when she was completely spent, did I allow myself to cum, filling her with everything I had.

ALICE

I woke up wrapped in Lucien's arms. He was sleeping soundly, his face turned to mine and he looked more handsome than I could have ever imagined, and with Lucien I imagined quite a lot. My body felt heavy from the love making, yet my head felt light and if I were daring enough to think it, I was happy.

I moved slightly, enough to nestle in closer to Lucien and shut my eyes tightly. I was so happy that it terrified me.

I finally understood why Lucien felt the way he did about relationships, but I still had to be completely sure that he was willing to give me one hundred percent of him. That it would not be an agreement but a relationship. There was so much baggage that came with him, a daughter he didn't see, a daughter who died and a wife. She was my biggest fear – that she would come back again and claim him as her own.

The pain of losing a child and to be so scared that it was because of one's own doing, was unimaginable. I couldn't believe that he would have been reckless with their lives, for someone like Lucien where everything was controlled and measured, to not be disciplined in his actions just didn't seem possible. *I was a different person back then.* A person couldn't change that much, could they?

I shifted slightly, moving the arm I was lying on before it went to sleep, and Lucien sighed softly and rolled over. The muscles in his back stood out against the tanned skin and I longed to stroke them, to memorise them, in case he went away again.

Knowing how easy it was for him to walk out on me in Paris, it troubled me that he could do the same here. I could wake up and he could be gone, off to find the family who had left him. I slid out of the bed, slipped on a tee—shirt and crossed the suite to the mini fridge. I'd no idea of the time but the sun was low in the sky, so I took a local lager from the fridge and opened it, checking on Lucien as the bottle-top hissed. When he didn't move, I put the bottle to my lips and drank down the cold drink. It tasted sweet and summery. I took it to the pool and, stripping naked, I lowered myself into the warm water and swam to the edge to look out over the tropical scene.

Was it right to feel this happy, despite the fears? Was it my time to find what I'd been looking for throughout my twenty-eight years? Did I finally deserve for all the pieces to come together? I put the beer on the side and lay floating on my back looking up at the cloudless sky. This was a place where feeling happy came with the scenery, the beautiful lush greens and bright blues, and I was, really happy.

And also very horny.

There was something about having a handsome, sexy, kinky man naked across the room that hit me right between the legs. I wondered if I would ever tire of feeling his touch, but I couldn't imagine it. Not ever.

I drained my beer and took another look at the dramatic view before swimming back across the small pool and climbing out. I dried myself off with a huge towel and padded across to the bed.

In his sleep, the dark shadows under Lucien's eyes had lightened and against his rested skin, his scar glistened silver. I ran my finger along it, feeling the knots underneath. Lucien's arm reached out and pulled me back into bed and tight against him. Softly I dusted my finger along his full lips. He scratched at them with his teeth and turned until his bare chest was fully facing me. The muscles, encased by warm, velvet skin, drew my touch and I traced them with my fingertips, watching his skin ripple. I followed the line of my fingers with soft, kisses, along the grooves of his ribs until I reached his hips. Lucien turned onto his back, his eyes still closed, and I kissed his chest, stroking his skin, and revelling in the delicious moans that came from him. His cock was standing up, straining towards me and I reached for it, gripping it in my palm and slowly rubbed up and down. The end glistened with pre-cum as Lucien began moving his hips, pushing harder into my hand. I felt the quiver in my pussy and the delicious release of juice as I took Lucien's hard cock in my mouth. He always tasted so good, the salty manliness coupled with the sharp shower gel he used, made my mouth water.

"Alice." Lucien groaned, grasping my head and thrusting against. "Fuck, you're so good at that. Don't stop, please, don't stop."

I didn't.

I sucked him hard, holding him to me with my hands on his hips. I needed to feel him, I had to know that I did *it* for him as much as he did *it* for me. Each drop of salty juice from him gave me everything I wanted, for that moment at least, until he pulled away and raised me above him, guiding his cock into my welcoming channel.

***

LUCIEN

It was the perfect way to be woken up, a beautiful woman pleasuring my cock with her luscious lips and with such enthusiasm that the blow job that led to a whole afternoon fucking in bed. Alice was insatiable and her endless cries of pleasure turned me on so much, my cock didn't soften at all.

I'd found my sexual match in Alice. The thrill of turning her on was an aphrodisiac in itself. It drove me crazy when she asked for me to fuck her harder and faster, and every time I tasted her sweet spot, and she cried out my name, I had to hold myself back from exploding onto the bed. She was open to exploring her sexual desires, and I was happy to guide her.

Occasionally, I caught worry in her eyes and it bothered me that I was the reason for it. I wasn't sure she was entirely trusting of me, which wasn't surprising given my past behaviour, but I felt it had more to do with the demon I brought into our relationship.

Relationship. The word sounded good and I rolled it over my tongue to savour the flavour of it. I'd avoided relationships since Isabelle left but to be in one again after a decade felt new and exciting. I was hopeful.

There had been a change to me since the morning, I could see it in my face. I'd slept more deeply in the few hours that Alice had been in the suite, than I'd done in years and to have her beside me meant I avoided the nightmares. Perhaps they would go now that I'd unburdened the darkness I carried. I hoped so, I needed to feel I was worthy of forgiveness because I still didn't know if it had been my fault.

It twisted my stomach every single time I thought about Ottie. I had brought the address to St Lucia with me, and somehow it felt as though Ottie had watched over me, giving me the backbone I needed to have come. Would I ever know if Ottie's death had been because of me? Alice didn't think so, but I had no real memories of that fateful afternoon, my own dance with death had wiped any recollection of the accident from my mind. The only person who could tell me the complete truth was Isabelle and she wholly blamed me.

The knife twisted in my gut when I thought about her. It was so good once, we were so happy, so glamourous, so envied but it all went to painfully wrong and then Ottie died. Anything that we had was shattered. Isabelle became vicious, my body was completely broken that I almost turned to stone lying in the hospital bed, and Hettie was caught in the middle. I missed my little girl. I missed her sweet smile and the way her arms used to wrap so tightly around my neck, as though she never wanted to let me go.

I had to find her.

I didn't want to cause any more damage to Hettie's life than she'd already had to repair, but I had to find her, she was the missing piece of my life and I wouldn't be whole until I knew where she was. I had no idea if Isabelle had poisoned her against me, or if Hettie had made her own choices, but I had to know. One way or the other, I had to know.

"You look far away!" Alice said, smiling gently as she crossed the room. Her hair was tousled and my stubble had left a red mark around her jaw.

"I was just thinking…"

"About?" The worried look came back and I reached for Alice's hand.

"I was thinking about Hettie."

Alice looked sad and then said, "you'll find her. I know you will."

"I hope so."

"I believe so!" She grinned. "When have you ever let a challenge beat you?"

I smiled at her. "Never."

"There you go!" Alice peered at herself in the mirror above my head. "Man alive, I look like the wild woman of the rainforest." She ran her fingers through her hair.

"You look gorgeous."

Alice opened her mouth to speak and promptly shut it again.

"Are you ok"? I asked, standing up from the chair and stretching my back.

"It feels all a bit too good to be true." She admitted, blushing. "I'm waiting for you to walk out of the room and not come back."

"I'm not going anywhere." I said, wrapping her in my arms. She felt tense and rigid. "I'm not, Alice. I'm not going anywhere. I want a relationship with you, I want to be with you. It took a lot to get to this point, but I'm not going anywhere for as long as you'll have me."

Alice's body relaxed and she rested her chin on my shoulder. "Ok." She said in a small voice.

"Ok?" I repeated pulling back and holding her by the shoulders. "Is it ok, or you feel ok or ok, I don't believe you?"

"It's ok!" Alice said, looking down at the floor. "It's all ok, every single bit of it."

"Even the bit where I turned up and fucked up your holiday?"

"Even that bit." Alice's stomach growled. "All the activity today has made me hungry!"

"Shall I call the butler?"

"No, let's eat at the beach. I can't spend all my hard-earned holiday in your room."

"Oh yes you can," I replied nuzzling into her neck and dropping light kisses along the underside of her jaw. Alice trembled against me. "Do you think you can wait ten minutes for food?"

"It depends what you have in mind!" She squealed as I scooped her up and took her back to the bed.

"I have kinky shit in mind."

I felt the heat in Alice's body as she leaned into me, her eyes closed. "What can I do for you, Sir?" She asked huskily.

"You can take off your clothes." I said as a hard tone crept into my voice. Damn it, I wasn't going to do this anymore, despite my *kinky shit* comment but Alice's willingness to play was too enticing. She did as I asked and then sat demurely on the edge of the bed, her eyes lowered to the floor. I could see her excitement, it was there in her hardening nipples and the faint movement in her thighs as the intimate muscles clenched. My cock stood up as I watched her growing discomfort. Knowing that I turned her on so much, just with a few words turned up my temperature. I just wanted to fuck her, to slide slowly into her hot, wet channel and own her until we both came, but she wanted the play and who was I to resist?

"Stand up." I barked. Alice's cheeks flushed and her tongue darted out to wet her bottom lip. I watched her breathing change, deepening as she waited with anticipation of what was to come. She wobbled a little as she stood up and waited, eyes lowered, her mouth open slightly. She had a tempting mouth, full red lips that quivered and I longed to kiss her. Instead I said, "turn around, put your hands behind your back."

I looked at her. Alice was standing, facing the open window, her hands clasped together behind her back. Her curves were soft and womanly with rounded buttocks sitting on top of slim, toned legs. She was the essence of a woman – beautiful, feisty, clever, strong, kind and as sexy as fuck. Her body was so perfectly shaped that I could have looked at her all day. Instead, I picked up the tied I'd discarded on the side table when I arrived and wrapped it around her wrists, pulling it tight. Alice gasped and trembled. Her willingness to perform like this made my cock strain painfully against my foreskin and I rubbed my hand up and the down the shaft in an attempt to relieve the pressure.

It didn't work.

The burning desire to be in Alice was unbearable. I tried to play the scene but my imagination and domination suffered under my craving for her. I did what I knew she liked. I took control, she submitted without question, lying down on the bed, arse raised, ready and waiting for the spank that was to come. When my hand made contact with her skin, the crack echoed around the room, followed by Alice's gasp of pleasure.

I looked at my hand print, red against the porcelain skin of her arse. Seeing it so vivid was a real turn on and I began to lose myself to the dominant side of me. I had no intention of being a Dom to Alice. I would not bring the violence to our sex life, she wasn't a plaything, she wasn't part of the scene that I'd turned my back on, this was for fun, for her desire and her needs, not mine. All I needed was to be with her. How she chose for that to happen, that was up to Alice.

I rubbed my hands over the cheeks of her arse and she tensed, waiting for my next move. Her pussy was swollen between her legs, and the silver trails of her sex were glistening on her thighs. I wanted to bury myself in her and lick every drop, instead I slowly ran my finger along her wet slit and when she moved her legs wider, I spanked her harder. It was my name she cried while she pulled at the ties on her wrists. She was at my mercy, face down on the bed and I spanked her in quick succession until her arse was red and her legs were drenched.

Alice moaned softly, a delightful sound that showed me I was doing exactly what she wanted. Her body was ripe and open, her pussy calling to my cock as I untied her hands. I didn't want her to feel any discomfort and my need for her was outweighing her need for this light bondage act.

"Lift yourself up." I said and she raised her torso from the bed. Her beautiful breasts hung low, nipples hard and rosy. I removed my own clothes, discarding them on the floor and said, "don't move."

I lowered myself onto my back and eased across the bed so I was lying under her. I sucked a nipple into my mouth and rolled my tongue around the bud. She always tasted so good. Sweet and floral and as I tugged on her nipple with my teeth, Alice tried to keep quiet, but she was as turned on as me. I took my time, sucking one then the other, pulling and nipping and tugging until she was cooing.

"Sit on the bed." I said and wriggled out from under her, crossing to the bathroom. I wanted to feel my cock between her glorious breasts and see her holding them together tightly, for me to enjoy. It was such a thrill the last time. I retrieved the body oil the hotel had left on the shelf and walked slowly back to the bed. Alice kept her face down as I wrapped my tie around her eyes, tying it securely and then liberally covered her with the expensive oil. I loved the feel of her slick breasts as I rubbed my hands over them. "Hold your tits together." I demanded and positioned my raging hard-on inside her cleavage. Alice did as I asked with a small sexy smile on her lips. It felt incredible. The warmth of her skin coupled with the sweet-smelling oil and the slickness that encased my cock was almost more than I could bear, and I came heavily into her open mouth.

"You are amazing." I whispered, untying the tie and throwing it down on the floor and pushing her back onto the bed, I said. "I'm going to show you how much."

ALICE

Our last night crept up on us without us even noticing. It had been the most wonderful holiday – when we managed to drag ourselves from Lucien's bed, we toured the island, climbed hills and mountains and swam in the gloriously warm aquamarine sea. Over the two weeks I'd allowed myself to fall more in love with Lucien than I thought would be possible. It terrified me. I feared what would happen when we returned to London. I had gotten used to the new Lucien - the calm, attentive, tender Lucien - and although I missed the endless dominance, the sex we had curled my toes and fried my brain.

Oh, we still did kinky shit, my red wrists and sore arse cheeks were testament to that, but somehow it increased the bond we had rather than diminish what our *agreement* had become – a relationship.

"Do you know that this is my first relationship in ten years?" Lucien said one morning in bed. "I'm practically born again."

My pussy was aching from some vigorous morning sex and wincing, I had gently rolled over to look at him. Running my finger across his lips, I said, "there is nothing 'born again' about you Lucien Ross!"

He'd laughed and we'd made love slowly, my tender areas wouldn't allow for more vigorous activities. Now I was lying on a near-empty Caribbean beach, our holiday almost over, thinking hack to the fierce, mind-blowing and raging hot sex that we'd had since we'd been here and then I wondered if it be the same at home? Would Lucien still want me with the obsessive focus that he did while it was just the two of us? Would his demons come back and take him from me?

Lucien was swimming in the sea, his strong arms sending rainbows across the ocean as he pulled himself along. I watched him from behind my glasses, sketching him as he swam. It was the perfect picture and my pencil skipped and swooped across the paper. Was I right to be fearful? In St Lucia we were able to hide from the world, hide from the churchyard in France, hide from the people we knew and hide from Isabelle. Here we could pretend that everything was normal.

Was it normal?

Normal people did normal things, they went to the supermarket and out for dinner and they hung out with their friends in wine bars on Saturday afternoons…

"Ah shit!" I sat up with my heart pounding against my ribs. It was all very well being wrapped up in each other four thousand miles from home, but if this was my new normal, I had one massive issue to face – how the fuck would I tell my friends about Lucien when none of them had any idea about him - and most fearsome of all, how would I tell Bonnie?

Lucien swam up the shore and walked out of the sea. He was perfection – broad shoulders, tight muscles and tanned skin – and I felt my mouth fall open as I stared at him. As much as I wanted to be cool, where Lucien was concerned, I failed miserably. He grinned as he clocked me staring at him.

"Like what you see?" He asked flexing his arms, grinning. We were the only people on the beach, so he pulled a few body-builder poses and I creased up laughing. Lucien flopped down next to me, his skin brown and glistening in the sun. To me, he was perfect. "Well," he asked, closing his eyes and throwing his arms behind his head, "do you?"

"Do I what?"

"Like what you see?"

I didn't just like what I saw, I loved it. I loved everything about the real side of him, the person he'd wanted me to see. I loved waking up with him and feeling his strong arms holding me close, I loved the feel of his body on mine but mostly I loved that he was more than I hoped a man could be. So, I replied with a casual shrug, "you'll do."

"You've always been a shit liar, Addison!" Lucien said, a knowing smile curving his lips. "I know full well that I do more than *you'll do* for you."

"Oh really?" I asked musically. "That just sounds like you have a huge ego…"

"I've got a huge something else too!" He said turning over to face me and winking. "See."

Lucien's erection was solid against his swim shorts and I felt the bubble of excitement in my stomach followed by the heavy feeling in my pussy. He was looking at me with a lascivious intent and my body began to swell and ripen. Lucien rolled over from his sun lounger and onto mine.

"I want to fuck you right here." He murmured in my ear. "Right on this five-star beach where anyone could see us."

"Do it then." I whispered back thickly. "Fuck me and let them see!" I moved onto my side and Lucien wrapped his body along mine, his erect cock digging into my back.

"You're shocking, Alice Addison!" Lucien rolled his tongue softly over my ear lobe and I felt my pussy muscles contract. He leaned over my and took my breast from my bikini top. My nipple sprang up as he rubbed his thumb across the sensitive nub and I felt his grin against my hair. "What if someone saw us," Lucien whispered into my ear, "what if they stood and watched you moving against my cock, your breasts on show, just like this." He flicked the string of my bikini and the top fell away from my breasts. "Would you like them to see you, to watch you cum?"

I took a hot breath in as my senses took over my body. Lucien knew my fantasy and was playing on my desires, offering up what I had once wanted. It had taken a moment of madness with Delphine to realise I enjoyed the fantasy as just that, but there, being on an empty beach, most of the hotel clientele were getting ready for dinner, I could indulge my fantasy. I could be anywhere. I lost myself in the images inside my head as Lucien, tantalisingly slowly, pulled my bikini bottoms aside and slid his long, hard length into me.

My intimate muscles tightened around him as he moved in and out of me, and the glorious stretch of my channel, as he entered me over and over, made me gasp each time. His hands never left my body, teasing my clit and my breasts until I was a shaking, shuddering mass of orgasm, the light erupting from me as the lava course around my nerves. Only when I had fully cum, did Lucien let himself go and fill me with his desire.

"You're so fucking hot." He said, nipping my ear. "I could fuck you all day."

"Shall we forget dinner?" I asked twisting to face him. "Shall we fuck all night instead?"

My stomach made an almighty growl and Lucien laughed, "I think your body has other ideas."

"Stupid body." I sulked. Lucien pulled me up and fastened my bikini top.

"Absolutely nothing stupid about it!" He nipped a nipple through the bikini and it sprang back up. "A very hot body, that I shall spend all night, post dinner, fucking."

"The whole night?" I said taking his hand and walking with him across the beach. "I'll hold you to that!"

LUCIEN

I wanted to be brave.

Alice squeezed my hand and whispered, "you can do it, Lucien. You can."

I wasn't sure I could. I felt sick. I felt guilty. I felt bereft. I felt loss. I felt the world closing in on me. Alice was standing by my side, her hand tight around mine. She must have felt the shaking in my palm but said nothing. Her quiet strength was the reason I had made it this far, to the gate on the edge of the churchyard.

It was so still on the other side of the gate, as though death had taken everything except for the gaudy flowers that were dotted across gravestones. My darling girl should not be there. She should be living her best life, falling in and out of love and in and out of friendships. She should be at university or travelling the world, not lying in a churchyard full of decay.

"I can't go in." I said numbly to Alice. "I can't do it. I put her there, how can I ever expect forgiveness for that?"

"You don't know that! Not for sure. But for now, Lucien, go and ask for the forgiveness you need because it will be there."

Her faith in me was unwavering. Alice had refused to believe I was responsible for Ottoline's death, she had more acceptance of me than I could ever deserve. I closed my eyes and tried to shut out the screams of agony that were trapped inside my head. I rubbed my finger along my scar, the permanent reminder of the tragedy I'd been a part of, always with me, always there to show me what I'd done.

"I don't believe it was your fault." Alice's words were barely audible under the pounding of my heart. I wanted to believe her, but I could remember, too clearly, the vitriolic words Isabelle had flung at me in the dark days that followed.

So much was my fault and there was so much to apologise for that I remained convinced I would be heading straight to hell.

Alice moved. It was a faint shift forward towards the gate. The panic that rose from my stomach took all feeling away from my hands and feet. "I can't do it, Alice. I can't go in." I was on the edge of an anxiety attack. The last one I had nearly killed me and would have done if not for Alice rescuing me. This time she was here, standing so close to me I could almost feel her heart beat, but I didn't think she could rescue me again.

I was back in the past where she couldn't reach me. The devil had his icy hand around my heart and whispered the words I hated the most. *You Killed Her.*

Alice dropped my hand and wrapped her whole body around mine until I was cocooned in her safety net. I don't know what I did to deserve her, the beautiful, kind, trusting person that she was. After everything I'd done, after the way I'd treated her, after all the shame I made her feel with my *agreement* nonsense she still let me in. She still wanted me. She still had faith in me. She had come here with me.

"You can do it," she whispered, "there is nothing to fear, only what you take with you. Leave it here. Go to Ottie." With one more tight squeeze Alice let me go. It was cold without the warmth of her body and I shivered. Alice handed me the small bouquet of yellow roses, Ottie's favourite and moved to hold the gate open for me.

"Will you be there when I come back?" I asked panicked. I was suddenly gripped by the fear that Alice wouldn't be there when I got back from Ottie, that she would see me for what I was and leave. I gripped her hand in my shaking palm.

"Always." She said, smiling gently. "I'll always be here." I took a step towards the gate, trying to shut out the devil standing beside me. I was terrified. I had only been that frightened once before, the night that Ottie died and I was too broken on the road to have been able to save her. I could hear her breaths fading, I could hear Hettie crying and Isabelle's panicked calls to me as she crawled along the road to reach Ottie. I could hear me begging God to make everything alright and the desperate offering of my soul to the Devil if he'd save her.

I don't know how I found the strength to walk through the church gate. I felt the agony of every bone that had broken as I walked slowly in, the gate banging on the catch behind me. Every unimaginable feeling I'd had in the last decade sliced through me and with each step I took, I knew that I was a man still so damaged even though the physical wounds had long since healed. I felt cold as I crossed onto the churchyard, a cold that was deep inside. Oh, God, Ottie I'm so sorry, I'm so sorry I put you here. The devil whispered, *Are you sure she wants to see you? You killed her after all.* Isabelle's voice, bitter and spiteful, 'you took my daughter away, you bastard, you stole my daughter from me...'

I turned to see Alice watching me, her hands tightly grasped in front of her. I heard my agonised cry and Alice dropped her bag to run to me as my legs buckled.

"Lucien." She said, cupping my face in her hands. "I'm here, I'm here." She kissed my face and held me close to her. "I'm here, you're not alone, you don't have to do this by yourself."

"I don't deserve you." I mumbled, gripping her hair in between my fingers. "For as long as I live, I'll never deserve you."

Alice said nothing, just kissed my mouth gently. I took control of myself and stood up, leaning on Alice as we took the final steps across the churchyard to Ottie's grave. It was tidy, someone had obviously been here very recently and had left flowers that had now faded. Alice took them from the vase and left me alone as she walked to the flower bin. I looked down at the small plot, the simple headstone with her name engraved and the dates, proof that she had been here once, for too short a time.

I sat down beside the grave, crossing my legs and leaning my face against the headstone I shed a decade of tears. Through those tears I told Ottie how much I loved her, how much I missed, how sorry I was for everything. I asked her to forgive me for taking her life away. My baby girl, the first person I'd ever loved with my whole being, was lying in the ground and it had all been my fault.

Time stood still as I sat with Ottie and when I finally moved, I was stiff and cold. I placed the flowers in the vase and stood up. I didn't want to leave her lying there alone, surrounded by strangers but there was no where else for her to be.

"I love you, Ottoline." I whispered, brushing the tears from my eyes. "Daddy loves you, my darling girl." I lay my hand on the cold head stone and turned away. I thought coming would be the hard part but leaving was so much worse.

I didn't look back at the small plot as I crossed the graveyard. The gate creaked as I opened it and looked for Alice. She was sitting on a bench where the evening sun was lingering. She looked up at me as I said her name, with so much love in her blue eyes that I wanted to tell her to run from me, that I was bad, she deserved someone better, instead I walked towards her and pulled her into my arms, burying my head in her floral scented hair.

"Thank you." I whispered. "Thank you so much."

ALICE

"I'm so jealous I feel sick." Bonnie said looking glumly at her bright pink cocktail. "I've been stuck with shagging Billy the Sandwich Man, because there is absence of hot men in London and all this time, you've been shagging Lucien. God hates me, I swear."

"It wasn't *all this time*," I said leaning over to squeeze her arm. "Really, it was about five minutes, then it ended and now…"

"And now you've been shagging him all over St Lucia!" Clare interrupted, grinning widely. "I bloody knew there was something going on with you two! How many times did I ask you, hey? How many! And you lied to my face, every single time."

I blushed shamefully. "I'm so sorry, Clare. I never lie, ever, it's one of my most hated hates but I did lie to you and I'm mortified about it. It's just, well…I suppose I was a bit embarrassed…it wasn't a relationship and didn't mean anything back then, well, I suppose it did to me, and maybe to him but…"

"I can't listen!" Bonnie said sitting up straight. "I can't listen to how you won the heart of the love of my life because I really like you and I may have to stop liking you if it all gets too gooey, so can I tell you about Billy the Sandwich Man instead?"

"No." Clare said picking up her glass. "No you can't because Billy is…well, he's Billy, he brings the sandwiches and I do not want any images of you shagging him."

"Last time I saw you, you said he was bad in bed and you were in hiding." I reminded Bonnie with an eyebrow raised.

"Well, Little Miss Secret Lucien Shagger, let me tell you that after the time I told you about, I accidentally got drunk and did it again…"

"Just the once?" Clare asked winking at me.

"Just a few times, actually." Bonnie said sheepishly, "and as it turns out Billy the Sandwich Man is a stallion between the sheets. I've never cum so much in my entire life, apart from my dirty fantasies about Lucien, but I suppose they'll have to stop now. Goddamn it!"

I laughed and then cringed, pulling a face. "Yeah, please stop because that would be weird."

"I'm still going to perv at him in the gym though." Bonnie told me smiling victoriously. "You can't stop me doing that!"

"Perv away!" I giggled. "Perv as much as you like. I perv every chance I get."

"Did you find out if there is the head of his ex-wife in his secret office cupboard." Bonnie asked. "It's still locked, you know!"

"I cannot imagine that Lucien would keep the head of an ex-wife in a cupboard, Bonnie, don't you think that would be completely psychopathic?"

"Have you seen inside the cupboard?"

"Well, no…"

"So how would you know?"

Before I could dwell on the secrets in Lucien's cupboard, Clare said, "it does explain why we had the first delivery of pastries this morning. I'd said last time we got them, he was shagging someone, now I know! You're the reason for pastries. Everyone was gossiping in the office as to where he was gone to, and Carol refused to tell anyone anything, even Lana which went down like a sack of shit. Can you imagine saying no to Lana? James in marketing told me that Carol got tipsy on sherry last week at an after-work drinks thing that Marketing put on, and let it slip that Lucien had been to St Lucia then to France. She never gets loose lipped but she was really pissed off because him going like that meant she had to cancel everything she'd arranged. Carol hates changing anything. She's bonkers!"

"So, he followed you to St Lucia then he took you to France?" Bonnie said looking a little green.

I nodded, not looking at her.

"Alice?" Bonnie asked.

"Yes Bonnie."

"Just so you know, you're off my Christmas card list."

"Ok."

"Are you sad?" She asked in a small voice.

"Very."

"Good." Bonnie grinned and stood up. She picked up her purse and said, "I feel inclined to get hammered now that the love of my life has gone forever. Same again?"

I don't remember getting home.

***

I woke early with an impressive headache and the nasty stale taste of alcohol in my mouth. It had been a fun evening, despite the ribbing I got from Bonnie and Clare over Lucien and it made Lucien's offer to move Addison Graphics into a spare office in Ross Industries that much more appealing.

I loved our corner of Shoreditch, but I had gotten back from St Lucia to a letter saying the rent was going up and it was pricing me out of the Hub. I wasn't the only one, the rumblings in the office suggested most were looking at relocating, but Saffron and I had only been there for such a short time that it felt as though a part of my big dream was slipping away.

I made a coffee and sat on the sofa looking through the paper at my options. Lucien's offer was vastly cheaper, but I wondered if it would make me feel like the little woman, taking charity from her man. I also wondered how I would get any work done, knowing he was just a floor below. It was bad enough when I tried to work from his apartment, it just ended with lots of sex and the job didn't get done, well it did but not the one I was being paid for! I chucked the paper in the bin and curled my legs under me.

The other option for Saffron and me was that we turned Xander's old room into an office, but the downside was that I could end up withdrawing from life again and Lucien could become my only link to the outside world.

I loved Lucien. Craved him. Desired him, but I also knew how it made me feel and I feared being lost in something that had more control over me than I had over it. As happy as I was in this new relationship, the mistakes of my past loomed scarily over me, and I was still painfully insecure about Isabelle.

Lucien refused to speak about her beyond what he'd told me in St Lucia, and I was too scared to ask anything further. Despite the affection he was now showing me, she was the third person in our relationship because she was the mother of his children, and for all I knew, he still loved her.

It made me more nervous than I cared to admit. I was blasé with Bonnie and Clare, over confident with my mother and gushing with Anna and Xander, but the truth was, I was terrified. My heart was fragile, and he could break it again in a heartbeat.

Then there was my other big issue. There was so much that Lucien wouldn't tell me, and I had so many unanswered questions that buzzed around my head like an irritating fly – Why did Isabelle come back? What did she say that nearly killed him that terrible day? I remembered the answering machine message I'd overheard the day he was taken to hospital. Had he listened to it too? And the most pressing question of all, did he still love her?

We may have been in a relationship, but he'd not uttered the three words that I longed to hear. I knew he wanted me, desired me and needed me – he said as much, I was the one he wanted to wake up with, but he was still holding back from me and it brought a different worry. Worry that Isabelle could take it all away.

He followed you to St Lucia, actions speak louder than words.

It didn't matter. I couldn't get Isabelle out of my head.

LUCIEN

I woke with a jolt from a horrific dream and rolled over, searching for Alice. Her warm, delicious body always chased the demons away, except that Sunday morning she wasn't there. I didn't like waking up without her, I'd gotten too used to her being in my bed, her naked curves wrapped around me and, if she woke before I did, I started the day with a huge erection that her beautiful mouth pleasured.

I grimaced and pulled the duvet over my head trying to ignore the echoes of the screams, the cries and Ottie's fading breaths that rang loudly in my silent apartment. They were the sounds I'd heard every night for ten years. I'd tried to bury myself in women, sex, dominance, business, whiskey – you name it, I tried it and then along came Alice and when she was there, the noises faded. Her belief in me made a difference but I could only silence the demons' whispers when she was with me. When I was alone, they could come for me and there was no escape. I hated them.

I rolled over and reached for my phone. I flicked on the TV news channel while I dialled her number and waited for her to answer. When she eventually picked up the phone I was engrossed in the report on parliament and the impeding election, feeling sick at the economic fuck up the government was causing. I knew Ross Industries would be alright, I had money in safe accounts, outside of the UK and there was no way I would watch my staff suffer financially in any political turmoil, but Alice's business was new, small and without spare capital, particularly as Alice had spent it on running from me.

It made me all the more determined for her to work from my spare office. At least I could give her work if her business slowed down.

"Hi." Alice answered with a smile in her voice. "You're awake early."

"So are you!" I replied, "I was expecting your answering machine. I was going to leave a dirty message about what I was planning on doing to you…"

"Oh?" She said breezily. I grinned as she tried to hide her interest. "And exactly what were you planning on telling my poor, innocent voicemail?"

"Well," I said, turning the news onto mute and lying back down in my bed with my arm behind my head. "I was just thinking about your gorgeous naked body and how much I'd like to see you tied to my bed, ready for me to do exactly what I wanted." I shifted and my cock stood up. "I want to tease you in all the ways you like, until your eyes start spiralling and you can barely see. I was thinking about the new toys I've bought and how much I'd like to use them on you…"

"New toys?" She whispered. I stroked the skin of my cock and a heaviness crept into my balls.

"Just for you." I murmured, squeezing my shaft as I spoke. I imagined it being Alice's hand, she knew exactly how I liked it. The end glistened with droplets of pre-cum as I enjoyed the slow self-pleasure. "I can hear your delicious moans as I use the flogger on you…"

"Flogger?" Her voice thickened as she saw in her head what I was imagining.

"Just for you, Alice. Soft suede, silk ties, those little stings that you like so much…"

"Fuck, Lucien…"

"That too." I said huskily. "I'm so hard Alice, it hurts. Are you wet just thinking about me doing this to you?"

"Yes." She was breathless when she spoke, and I felt a tightening in my groin. I rubbed my cock faster as I continued to speak.

"Are you touching yourself?"

"Yes."

"Do you know what happens to dirty girls?" I'd not called her that in a long time, I wasn't sure she liked it, but at that moment, with my cock in my hand, knowing she was stroking herself, I was being swept along in the moment.

"Yes." She whispered, her breath ragged.

"They get punished."

"I know."

"Alice, I do not give you permission to cum, do you understand?"

"Yes."

"I'll send a car." I cancelled the call and used an app to arrange a car. I didn't finish myself off, instead I went for a shower and mentally planned the pleasure Alice was going to receive.

I was still rock hard when the doorbell went.

***

"I don't believe it." I felt the blood drain from my body and pool at my feet.

"Hello Lucien."

Isabelle was standing in front of me, her face like stone. She had an envelope in one hand and a mobile phone in the other. The large diamond on her ring finger glinted in the light, throwing rainbows over her thin hand.

I shook my head in disbelief. "You're here?"

"Obviously." She snapped, pushing past me and walking into the flat. Numbly I followed her. "I've had enough now, Lucien, it's time things were sorted out. I asked you six months ago…"

"Where's Hettie."

"Never mind where Hettie is, she's safe from you."

It was a blow to the stomach, cutting deeper than a knife could go.

"I want to see her." I demanded feeling a panic rise from my belly. The woman standing in front of me was a stranger, I saw nothing of the Isabelle I once knew in her face. She was thin, pinched, and glaring at me as though she wished I was dead.

"Hettie doesn't want to see you. She wants nothing to do with you." Isabelle waved the envelope at me and said, "I want you to sign the papers. It's time we all moved on."

"You want a divorce? Fine, but I want to see my daughter before I sign anything."

Isabelle shook her head slowly. "Do you really think she wants to see you? After everything that's happened."

"I have rights…"

"You have no rights at all." Isabelle snapped, her face reddening.

"She is my daughter." I shouted, feeling intense anguish tightening in my chest. "She is a part of me, the only part I have left, and you took her away when I was lying in a hospital bed. I was dying, Isabelle, and you took her away. Do you have any idea what that did to me?"

"I did what I had to do to protect Hettie."

"You did it to pay me back." I said, wrapping my arms around myself and closing my eyes against the pain her words were causing. "You wanted to pay me back for everything that went wrong…"

"You were never there, Lucien…."

"I was building the business, Isabelle, building a life for us. I should have been with you in France more, I thought the weekends would be enough. It was the wrong decision and you told me often enough…" I shook my head as she glared at me. I could hear all the arguments, the nasty name calling and the breaking hearts of emotionally distant people. "I wanted to give you what you'd never had, and I got it wrong."

"I wanted my husband…"

"No, you didn't! Maybe in the beginning but then you stopped caring if I was there or not, as long as you got the things you wanted, Isabelle. You loved the lifestyle but the more I gave to you, the more we lost in the process…Please

Isabelle, I want to see Hettie, I *need* to see Hettie. You cannot keep her from me, it's been ten years…I'm her father."

"Jean-Claude is her father now…"

"Jean-Claude? You don't mean Jean-Claude, my closest friend…the man who saved my life? Not him? Anyone else but, Jesus, Isabelle, tell me it's not him…" Jean-Claude was our closest neighbour in France and quickly became my best friend. He was a world-famous surgeon but that aside, he was the kind of friend a man needed – solid, dependable and completely trust-worthy. He put me back together after the accident, but healing took a long time and he had moved to work in Switzerland before I'd been discharged. We lost touch and perhaps I should have tracked him down, but I buried myself in bad choices and by the time I came out the other side, it was too late.

"Yes." Isabelle snapped. "He is the man I'm going to marry, and he is the only father that Hettie needs. He's been there for her …"

"Because you took her away." I sat down heavily on the sofa. "I should have been there for her, but you took her and, in doing that, you destroyed what was left of me. I won't sign the papers until I see Hettie. How long after you left me did you get together with Jean-Claude?"

Isabelle took the papers from the envelope and flung them onto the coffee table. "Just sign the fucking papers Lucien and let me get back to my life."

"Can you at least answer my question?"

"My life is none of your business, Lucien."

ALICE

I was so horny I could barely climb the stairs to Lucien's apartment. Every part of me was on fire and the weight in my belly was getting lower and lower with each step. By the time I reached his floor, I was glowing with a need for kinky, that I felt certain I would be unable to hold my orgasm back.

For which I'd be punished.

My stomach flipped.

It'd been a long time since I'd indulged in the really kinky side to me. Lucien had occasionally spanked me or controlled our activities, but this was a part of me that he'd unleashed when I had no idea it had even existed inside me, and I was desperately excited to play. I was so hot for him that I could smell my own desire and see the sparks dancing over my skin. As I reached his door, I could hear the angry voices on the other side. Lucien and one other.

Isabelle.

Lucien's front door was ajar, so I stood beside the gap, barely breathing as my heart deafened me with its anxious beat.

"Can't you just listen to reason?" Isabelle shouted. I took a deep breath in and tried to calm myself. If they were angry then maybe I had nothing to fear, but anger was passion and that turned to...*Stop it, Alice, stop thinking.*

"Reason? You turn up, out of the blue, after ten years and ask me to be reasonable? You've got a nerve, Isabelle."

"Sign the papers, Lucien. Sign them and I'll leave, you won't have to see me again, I can move on...you can finally move on!"

"I had." Lucien said. I stopped breathing. What did he mean, *I had*? "I had finally moved on. Seven months ago, the fog had begun to clear, and I was getting to a good place. Then you text me in the middle of the night and I threw everything away to come back to London because you were wanted to talk."

"Oh, I'm sorry," she said sarcastically, "did I drag you away from one of your many sluts?"

I heard him take a sharp breath and I moved a little closer to the gap. "What are you talking about?"

"I know about them all, Lucien. All the women, all the cheap sluts you picked up. I know about them all, husband dearest."

"Have you been spying on me?"

"I did what I needed to…"

"All this time and you were watching me? Why?"

"In case I needed something, and you wouldn't give it to me, like now. There was one that surprised me, though, the brunette. The one you were seeing when I last came to London. She isn't your usually type Lucien. I'd imagined she was another temporary fuck…"

"You leave her out of this. This is about you and me, not anyone else, especially her."

"It's about all of it, Lucien." Isabelle snapped. "I want a divorce because I've waited long enough…"

"You've waited? What do you think I've been doing, Isabelle? Waiting, that's what! Waiting for you to come back and bring Hettie, yet there has been nothing from you apart from your impromptu arrival here last year. You can't want to marry him that much if you've waited until now. You left me ten years ago, Isabelle, you left me in a hospital bed, and you didn't even look backwards…I had no idea where you were and trust me, I have searched and searched for you. You took everything and didn't even leave a note. And now you've decided to come back, bringing all this hatred with you, demanding a divorce…"

"You have the same hatred…"

"I did." Lucien said suddenly quiet. "For so long, I hated both of us. I had so much hate, it ate me up. Yes, there were women, lots of them, distractions from the voices in my head. I'm not apologising for them, if that's what you're after." I heard him sigh. "You can have your divorce, Isabelle. I've spent too long regretting you, but the adoption papers, no, I won't sign those, and you have no right to ask me."

"I have every right…."

"Until Hettie tells me herself that she wants a new father and a new last name, I'm not signing a fucking thing." He snapped.

"She won't talk to you."

"One day, she will. Once she realises that you've spent the past decade poisoning her." Isabelle laughed mirthlessly as Lucien said, "God only knows how hard I tried to find you, I searched the entire planet, I had teams of people looking for you…"

"You obviously didn't look hard enough."

"You will never know what I did, or what I went through, because you chose not to." Lucien said, his voice full of regret. "You will never know how much you tore me apart, piece by piece, when you left. God, if you had any idea…It wasn't just you who lost someone that day, it was me too, I lost Ottie and I lost you. You were my love Isabelle."

I moved slightly and could just about see Lucien sitting on the sofa with his head in his hands. He raised his face to Isabelle who was standing back, his features stricken. I felt my stomach free fall to the floor as I looked at the sadness on his face. I wanted to barge my way in and claim him for myself, push Isabelle away and shut the door on the world. I swallowed the nausea that was burning my throat and waited.

"That afternoon was so perfect, do you remember? It was like old times, before we had anything except each other. We were so much happier when we were poor, weren't we? I was watching you laughing and thinking how much I wanted to make things right, for you and me to get back what we had before it all went wrong. There was something between us, a moment, a flicker and I know you felt it too…"

"I did feel it." Isabelle said, her voice suddenly soft. "Just for a moment we were 'us' again, I don't know how it happened, it just did, but it didn't last long and then it was gone."

"It could have been so different." He said, his voice breaking, and I suddenly felt hot tears on my cheeks. I wondered how long I'd been silently crying for. I felt certain I was watching the end of my happiness. I swallowed a sob and shut my eyes.

"We got too lost, Lucien." she admitted. "Even a perfect moment can't last. I don't think our marriage would ever have lasted. Is that what you were hoping for? That we would one day find our way back? I thought you would have moved on by now."

"I'm trying too." He said bleakly. "And now you're here and it's opened up the wounds all over again…" Then I heard Lucien beg. "Please Isabelle, I want to see Hettie."

"She's not here, Lucien, it's just me."

There was a long silence and I bit my lip waiting for one of them to speak.

"After last year, I didn't think I'd ever see you again." Lucien said finally.

"I had to see you."

"Why? To stick the final knife in?"

"I didn't think you'd feel anything for me anymore." Isabelle paused and then said. "Do you still love me, Lucien?"

There was a long pause and I bit down on my lip so hard I drew blood. Somewhere a clock was ticking, loudly, counting the seconds of the silence until Lucien said in a voice filled with emotion, "Oh, Isabelle, it was always you…"

I didn't wait to hear anymore. I span on my heels and ran down the stairs, pushing open the door with a bang. I stopped running when I could no longer breathe. Was that it? Was it over? Had Isabelle been calling the shots all along?

With my heart slowly crumbling inside my chest, I took the underground home towards a future I could no longer see.

TO BE CONTINUED ...

IVORY

The final instalment in the Addison-Ross Saga is Coming Soon

Keep your eye on my social media for all updates for the release of Ivory!

Facebook – Katie Jane Newman
Facebook Page - @KatieNewmanAuthor
Instagram - @katiejanenewmanwriter
Twitter - @KJNewmanAuthor
Website – www.katiejanenewman.co.uk

Authors note – mistakes? Very likely! Sorry!

***

**A million thanks, as ever, to my fabulous test readers:
Amanda, Beth, Cinzia, Kate and Nicola - you girls are the very best!**

**Special Thanks to Leah W.
Your hard work is more appreciated than you'll ever know.**

Printed in Poland
by Amazon Fulfillment
Poland Sp. z o.o., Wrocław